HERO

RESCUE MISSION

HERO
RESCUE MISSION

JENNIFER LI SHOTZ
#1 *New York Times* bestselling author

HARPER

An Imprint of HarperCollins*Publishers*

Hero: Rescue Mission

alloyentertainment
Produced by Alloy Entertainment
1325 Avenue of the Americas
New York, NY 10019
www.alloyentertainment.com

Library of Congress Control Number: 2017949431
ISBN 978-0-06-256047-6 (trade bdg.)—ISBN 978-0-06-256045-2 (pbk.)

17 18 19 20 21 CG/LSCH 10 9 8 7 6 5 4 3 2 1

❖

First Edition

For our sweet pup, Vida, and for all the beautiful rescue dogs out there waiting for a home. Your family is coming!

1

HERO PACED BACK AND FORTH IN the stands. His tail was up at attention, and his eyes were locked on Ben.

Ben stole a look at his dog from the infield and shook his head in astonishment. He could swear that somehow the black Labrador seemed to understand that this game really mattered—and that Ben's team was losing.

It was the game leading up to the playoffs—the most important game of the season so far—and Ben's team, the Tigers, was down by three runs. It was now the top of the ninth inning, and the other team was up.

Ben was nervous. If they lost this game, their season was over.

The tension was thick at the baseball field. Hundreds of parents and brothers and sisters filled the bleachers and shivered in the light fall breeze, anxious looks on their faces. The crowd waited for the next batter to step up to the plate. It felt like everyone was collectively holding their breath.

From his position at shortstop, Ben surveyed the diamond, squinting into the setting afternoon sun. The other team had two guys on base, but they also already had two outs. They just needed to get the next batter out fast so Ben's team could get up to bat.

Then, if Ben's team could score, maybe they could tie up the game and go into extra innings.

But that was a big *if*.

Ben looked into the stands. His mom stood with her hand shading her eyes, scanning the other team's dugout—probably sizing up the other players. She looked like she wanted to march right in there and tell them off. Ben's little sister, Erin, stood next to their mom, her face scrunched up in frustration. She wanted Ben's team to win pretty badly.

Ben's dad was the assistant coach. He stood by their dugout, calm and still, his lips pressed together in a half smile. A couple of feet away, Scout, the mutt puppy, sat patiently, watching Ben's dad's every move with big, observant eyes.

Scout was Ben's dad's shadow these days. Where one went, the other followed. Training Scout was a round-the-clock activity that they both lived and breathed.

Ben's dad—Sergeant Dave Landry of the Gulfport, Mississippi, police force—was training Scout for K-9 duty. One day, Scout was going to be a rescue dog just like Hero, and Ben couldn't have been prouder.

Hero and Ben had found Scout when he was a tiny puppy who had escaped from a dogfighting ring. Ben's friend Jack had raised Scout. Then everyone realized that Scout had the potential to be an amazing search-and-rescue dog—just like Hero. Scout just needed some training, and Sergeant Landry was the man for the job.

Jack had been sad to give up Scout, but he also wanted Scout to be happy—and Scout was happiest when he was working.

Ben's dad gave Scout the signal to lie down, and the pup put his head between his paws, wagging his spotted tail. His big, pointed ears perked up, ready for his next command.

Ben shook out his arms and hopped up and down on his toes a few times. He looked at his best friend, Noah Mazer, who stood on the pitcher's mound. Noah turned and nodded at him. Then Ben looked over to his left at Jack, who played first base. Jack tipped the brim of his cap toward Ben in salute.

Ben turned to see who was coming up to bat and groaned. The kid had to be close to six feet tall, and he was sturdy, with muscular arms and a thick neck. He smirked, like he knew he was bumming out his opponents just by showing up.

Noah calmly wound up for the pitch. Things started to move in slow motion. The ball left Noah's hand and sailed in a smooth line toward the batter. The batter's expression shifted from cocky to confused as the ball arced slightly upward and then—almost invisibly—changed its path.

The big guy at home plate screwed up his face, flexed his muscles, and swung hard. Ben waited for the crack of bat and ball. He bent his knees, poised to jump and run the second he spotted the ball coming his way . . . but nothing happened.

The batter's swing propelled him in a full circle. He

4

spun around awkwardly.

"Strike one!" cried the umpire.

Ben held his breath. Noah threw two more curveballs, and the umpire called two more strikes.

The batter stood at home plate for a second, failing to understand how he had missed the third curveball. But he had—and Ben's team was up.

"Woooohoo!" Jack howled as he ran toward Noah.

"Noah!" Ben screamed as he jumped on his friend. "That was insane!"

Ben, Noah, and Jack jogged to the dugout. The rest of their team pounced on Noah, cheering and calling his name.

"MAZER, MAZER!" They punched Noah on the shoulder and rubbed his hair to congratulate him.

Noah grinned but tried to wave away his unruly teammates. "Come on, guys—we still have to score! We're still, you know, losing and all."

"Noah's right, team," Ben's dad said. "Let's focus."

The team quieted down. They gathered around him in a half circle.

Coach Lee hunched in the corner, studying his clipboard and furiously scratching at a piece of paper with a pencil before the next inning.

"Noah, that was some great pitching," Ben's dad said. "You dug deep and it worked."

Ben gave Noah a high five.

"You guys just got a break—let's take advantage of it," Ben's dad went on.

"We're still three runs down," said a kid in the back.

"You're down," Ben's dad said matter-of-factly, "that's true. But you wouldn't be the first team to come up from behind and win the game. So let's get out there and show 'em what we can do, okay?"

"Okay," the boys responded.

"Come on," Ben's dad said, clapping loudly. "You can do better than that. Let me hear you."

"Okay!" the boys shouted, grins breaking out on their faces. They started to get pumped up again, chattering and cheering loudly.

Ben's dad leaned in to Ben. "You know what you have to do, right, kid?"

"I do," Ben said. "Breathe. Focus. Stay in the moment."

"That's right."

His dad clapped him on the shoulder, and Ben

stood a little taller in his uniform. He had been batting fourth the whole game, but batting fourth in the ninth inning was a lot of responsibility. If the three batters ahead of him got on base, *Ben* could be the person to win the game.

"Okay, team," Coach Lee called from across the dugout. He walked over. "Jack, Noah, Marwan, you guys are up first." Coach Lee added, "Ben, I'm counting on you to bring it home."

Ben nodded even as his stomach churned with nerves.

"You got this, Ben," his dad reassured him. "It's just you and the pitch, okay? Keep your eye on the ball and breathe."

"Okay." Ben took a slow, deep breath. "Thanks, Dad." He exhaled.

Ben was up.

He couldn't believe it: Jack, Noah, and Marwan had all gotten on base. The only hitch had come when a foul ball had barreled toward Noah and hit him in the arm—hard. Noah had yelped in pain, and Coach

Lee had called a time-out and jogged over.

Noah and the coach had conferred for a moment, and from his spot in the dugout, Ben saw Noah shake his head. He was trying to convince the coach he was fine, but Ben could tell even from across the diamond that his friend was in a ton of pain.

With a grim look on his face, Coach Lee had trotted back toward the dugout and the game had resumed.

Now the families in the bleachers were going wild with excitement—hooting and hollering like they were at the World Series.

Ben's heart pounded hard in his chest. His palms were sweaty as he gripped the bat and stepped toward home plate. The roaring of the crowd faded into the background, and all he heard were the sounds of his own breathing, his mom shouting "GO, BEN!" and Hero barking excitedly.

It's just you and the pitch, he heard his dad's voice in his head say. *Breathe.*

Ben eyed the pitcher carefully, taking in his posture, his expression, and his fingers curled around the ball. The pitcher wound up, drew his arm back, and twisted his body around. The ball flew out of his hand, and Ben watched it move toward him.

He swung as hard as he could. He felt the power in his arms and wrists, and he focused on the follow-through, like his dad always reminded him. He felt the connection between bat and ball before he heard it—a vibration that shot up his arm and into his shoulders. He watched in amazement as the ball sailed up, up, up, and out. All the outfielders tipped their heads back to watch the ball as it flew over them.

Ben froze at home plate, the bat dangling from his left hand. Surely one of the outfielders was going to catch the ball, he thought. There was no way it was going to keep going, right?

But it did. The ball disappeared over the fence.

Home run!

"Run, Ben!" Coach Lee called from the sidelines.

"Run, Ben!" Ben's mom screamed from the bleachers.

Ben ran, a giant grin on his face, chasing Jack, Noah, and Marwan around the bases until they all piled onto home plate together, cheering and high-fiving one another while their teammates howled with joy in the dugout.

Somehow, they'd won the game. Unbelievable.

2

BEN LOOKED INTO THE CHEERING CROWD. His mom and sister were jumping up and down, shouting his name and clapping. Hero's snout was tilted up toward the sky, and he was barking excitedly.

But where was his dad?

Ben searched for him in the dugout. His dad wasn't there. And neither was Scout. Ben's excitement about his home run—and winning the game—was replaced with confusion.

He scanned the crowd, but his view was obstructed by the swarm of teammates who surrounded him, chanting his name and fist-pumping the air.

"Landry!"

"Way to go, Landry!"

"Go, Ben!"

Ben high-fived his teammates, but he was distracted. He stood on his toes to scan the crowd. Finally, he spotted his dad.

He was in the parking lot, his phone pressed to his ear. There was a serious expression on his face.

He hadn't even seen Ben hit the home run and win the game.

But Ben knew enough about his dad not to be upset. When you grow up with a dad on the police force, you learn that work always comes first. This time it looked like something really big was happening.

Scout sat patiently by the car. He was already wearing his yellow vest with GULFPORT POLICE K-9 written across it in big block letters. Just like Ben's dad, Scout was ready for action.

"Dude!" Noah shouted, punching him on the shoulder and drawing his attention back to the team. "That was amazing! We won!"

"Great hit, Landry," Coach Lee called out.

"Thanks, Coach." Ben grinned.

Ben glanced back toward the parking lot. His dad was off the phone and climbing into his car.

Noah followed Ben's gaze and understood what was happening right away. "You okay?" Noah asked as the rest of the team kept cheering.

"Yeah." Ben tore his eyes from his dad and turned to look at his friend. "But how's your arm?"

"Not sure . . . it still sort of hurts." Noah frowned and rubbed his elbow.

"Your dad's leaving?" Jack pushed through the crowd toward them.

"Looks like it. Must be something big down at the station."

"Must be," Noah said.

Ben gathered up his stuff and headed to the bleachers, his ears still ringing from the celebration.

His mom gripped him tightly in a hug. Erin wrapped her tiny arms around his waist. Hero jumped up and put his front legs on Ben's back, yelping excitedly.

"Congratulations, honey!"

"You did it, Benny!"

Ben let them hold on to him for a moment, but there was only one thing on his mind.

"Where's Dad?" he asked. "Why did he have to leave?"

Something flickered across his mom's face—was it fear? Ben couldn't be sure. She composed herself and looked him right in the eye.

As Ben had gotten older, his parents had always tried to tell him the truth about his dad's work—as much as they could, anyway. It was a fact of life that Ben's dad faced danger every day.

"Well," his mom said simply, "there's a pretty bad case happening right now, Ben."

Ben swallowed the lump in his throat.

"Two convicts escaped from prison," she went on, lowering her voice so Erin couldn't hear all the details. "They were last seen outside Gulfport, so they called up all the K-9 teams in the area. Your dad and Scout are heading up the search."

Hero's ears flicked at the sound of Scout's name. He wedged himself between Ben and his mom, sat down, and looked up at them, listening. Ben dropped his hand to his dog's neck and scratched him beneath the collar.

"Are they . . . ?" Ben faltered. "Are these guys dangerous? What were they in for before they escaped?"

His mom sighed and shook her head a little. "Nothing good. Let's leave it at that."

"What are you guys talking about?" Erin asked, tugging on the sleeve of Ben's sweatshirt. His heart was pounding, but he forced a smile onto his face.

"We're talking about the fact that you're going to buy me ice cream to celebrate!" Ben said, his voice extra bright.

"Oh, Benny," Erin said, crossing her arms. "You're so silly. You know I don't have enough money for that."

"Oh no!" Ben cried in mock horror. "No money for ice cream? That's terrible!"

"Tell you what," his mom said, "it's my treat!"

"Yay!" Erin shouted.

They headed toward the car. Hero trotted alongside them while Ben held Erin's hand and exchanged worried looks with his mom. A cell phone jingled in Ben's mom's purse. She fished it out, spoke into it for a quick second, then handed the phone to him.

"Your dad wants to talk to you, Ben."

"Hi, Dad—where are you? Is everything okay?" Ben could tell by the background noise that he was driving in his squad car.

"Congratulations, buddy!" his dad shouted into the phone. "I'm so proud of you guys—you worked really hard for this, and you deserve it."

"Thanks, Dad." Ben felt an urgent need to ask his dad questions about the case. "Do you know where the convicts are yet?"

"Everything's fine," his dad reassured him. "I'm just really sorry I wasn't there to see your home run and to see you guys win. But we'll celebrate when I get back, okay?"

"Okay, Dad. Thanks."

"Listen, pal, I need you to do something for me."

"Anything."

"I need you to look out for your mom and Erin tonight, okay?"

Ben felt unsteady on his legs. Something in his dad's voice sounded different. Almost . . . worried. Was there something his dad wasn't telling him? "Okay," Ben managed to say. "But, Dad—"

"I have to go now, Ben," his dad interrupted. "Can you pass the phone back to Mom? I love you."

Every instinct in Ben's body told him not to let go of the phone. He wanted to keep his dad talking, but he knew he had no choice. He had to say good-bye. "I love you too, Dad. See you soon."

His mom held out her hand for the phone, then stepped out of earshot. Ben opened the back door of the car for Erin, and she scrambled into her booster seat.

Just then, Noah and his parents walked up. Noah was cradling his right arm in his left and looking miserable. Hero ran over and snuffled at him.

"Hey, Hero," Noah said glumly. Hero cocked his head and gave Noah a curious look, like he was trying to figure out what was wrong with him.

"Ben!" Noah's mom said. "What a great hit!"

"Nice game, Ben," Noah's dad said, clapping him on the back. "So proud of you boys."

"Thanks, Mr. and Mrs. Mazer," Ben said. He looked at Noah and noticed the bulge of an ice pack stuffed into the sleeve of his friend's shirt. "Uh, dude," Ben said, pointing at Noah's arm. "What's happening?"

Noah grimaced. "What's happening," he said, sounding despondent, "is that they think I might have a hairline fracture from that foul ball, and Coach said I can't play again until I get cleared by the doctor. But I think it's just a bruise." He tried to straighten his arm to prove his point, but even that slight movement made him wince.

Hero raised himself up on his back legs and nudged gently at Noah's arm.

"Hero, down!" Ben commanded the dog. "Noah's hurt." Hero got down.

"It's okay," Noah said. "He's just trying to make me feel better."

"Good boy," Ben said as Hero sauntered back over and sat down by the car. "You're just giving Noah a checkup, huh?"

But Ben didn't have the heart to tell Noah the truth: Hero was also trained to recognize serious injuries. And he was never wrong.

3

THAT EVENING, BEN, HIS MOM, AND Erin were sitting around the dinner table when the phone rang. Ben jumped up to grab it, hoping that it was his dad with news that he'd be home soon. But instead, it was the last person he expected: Coach Lee.

"Ben, I'm glad I caught you. Listen, I think you should know that Noah's arm—that's a serious injury he's got there."

Ben nodded, his brow furrowing. "Yeah, Coach, I could tell. Is he going to be okay?"

"Well, that's the thing, Ben. I'd say there's no way he's going to be able to play in the next game," Coach Lee's voice was heavy with worry.

Ben's mom looked up from the dinner table and raised her eyebrows. Ben shook his head.

"But . . ." Ben started to say as the coach's words sunk in. "But that's the first game of the playoffs. We can't play without our pitcher, right?"

"That's what I'm calling about, actually. Just the other day, your dad and I were saying that your arm's gotten really strong these past couple of months. What do you think about pitching the next game?"

"Wait—what?" Ben wasn't sure if Coach Lee was joking or not. He started to laugh, then realized the coach was totally serious. "But I'm not a pitcher! I mean, what about Joey?"

"Joey's a solid backup pitcher." Coach Lee paused. "But he's not ready to start in a playoff game. I've had my eye on you for a few weeks."

"But I can't—it's just a few days away. I have to play shortstop . . ." Ben trailed off, clutching the phone.

Ben wished the world would slow down for just one second. His head was spinning with everything that had happened today. The thrill of hitting a home run and winning the game was all mixed up with his disappointment that his dad hadn't been there to see it. And now he was full of nerves—for Noah and for himself. How could he be ready to pitch such an important game in just a few days? And how would that make Noah feel?

There was only one person Ben wanted to talk to about all this: his dad.

But his dad wasn't there.

"I know, Ben," Coach Lee said in response to Ben's silence. "I know it's a lot all at once. But I need someone who can keep cool under pressure."

Ben swallowed. "Are you sure, Coach?" Hero came up beside Ben and nudged his wet nose into Ben's hand.

"I'm positive."

The next morning, a Saturday, three seriously bummed-out boys and one helpful dog were gathered in Ben's front yard. It had been completely replanted since the hurricane, and the grass was still coming in. Jack was already muddy from playing fetch with Hero.

Ben tossed the baseball up and down, while his best friend sat slumped over on a deck chair, his very swollen arm cradled in a sling. Hero sniffed around their feet, then rested his chin on Noah's leg.

"Let's get this over with." Noah sighed.

He looked miserable. Noah had spent the night in the emergency room, where an X-ray had revealed that he really did have a stress fracture in his arm.

Noah was going to miss the playoffs completely.

Ben felt awful too. He hated taking Noah's place, but he didn't have a choice.

"We don't have to practice now," Ben said.

Noah shot him a look of horror. "This game is less than a week away, and trust me, you need all the help you can get."

"You may be injured," Ben said, "but you're still hilarious."

"Don't worry, Noah. We're only going to program Ben to win the playoffs. Then we'll deactivate his pitching skills for good and you can have your position back," Jack joked.

"Thanks, Jack." Noah shifted in his seat, wincing as he moved.

Jack crossed to the far end of the lawn, and Ben swung his arm in a circle a few times to warm it up. Before today, he had never pitched for real before—only when he was practicing with Jack and Noah or throwing a tennis ball to Hero.

Ben's stomach was tied in knots. He didn't feel

confident about pitching, he didn't feel right that he was stepping on his best friend's toes, and, worst of all, he still hadn't been able to talk to his dad about any of it.

Because his dad hadn't come home last night.

The last Ben and his mom had heard from Ben's dad was when he texted a little after midnight. *All good,* the message said. *We're getting close. Love you. Kiss the kids for me.*

They knew that "getting close" meant he and Scout were closing in on the two escaped convicts. But hours had passed since then, and they hadn't heard a word.

Around 6 A.M., Ben had turned on the local news and flipped from station to station. The reporters all said the same thing: The convicts were still at large.

His dad had been on so many risky cases before, but for whatever reason, this time was different. Ben felt it, and he could tell his mom did too—though neither one of them wanted to admit it to the other.

There was nothing to do but wait. And pitching was the perfect distraction.

"Let's get on with it," Noah said drily.

"Ready when you are, Ben," Jack said.

Ben shifted his weight onto his back foot, turned his body sideways, and pulled up his knee. He drew his arm back and fired a ball right at Jack. It landed with a satisfying *thwack* right in the leather pocket.

"Nice," Jack said.

"Decent," Noah said with a shake of his head. "But you need to pull your arm back more."

Hero pranced over to Jack, stuck his muzzle into Jack's mitt, and gently took the ball in his mouth. He carried it over to Ben. Ben wiped the slobber off on the leg of his jeans.

Ben threw again.

"Better," Noah said. "Now release a second sooner."

Ben released sooner and turned to Noah for feedback while Hero retrieved the ball again.

"Not bad. Release it at the same time, but let your fingertips feel it for, like, a millisecond more."

Ben wasn't quite sure how exactly he was supposed to do that, but he bit his tongue and tried again. They went on like this for more than an hour, with Noah seemingly making up tiny corrections and dishing them out. Ben was tired, but he was finally starting to get into the zone. Hero was getting a workout too, dashing between Jack and Ben in an endless loop.

Ben wound up for another pitch, but before he could release the ball, something caught his eye.

It was a patrol car moving slowly down the block.

Ben let his arm fall to his side and held the ball loosely in his hand. Noah and Jack froze.

Hero barked once, then ran over and sat down, leaning against Ben's leg.

A horrible feeling washed over Ben—some grim combination of numbness, fear, and despair. He had never allowed himself to really contemplate the *what ifs* of his dad's job, but he was the son of a cop. Every day was a risk. Every day could mean danger.

But maybe today was the day that danger became a reality.

As the car drew closer, Hero moved in front of Ben, his ears up and his body on alert. He watched the car approach. Hero was guarding Ben, protecting him, as if he could stop the worst kind of news from arriving.

The patrol car turned slowly into the Landrys' driveway and came to a stop.

4

BEN INHALED SHARPLY AND STEADIED HIMSELF. Blood pounded in his ears; the grass beneath his feet and the sunlight and trees overhead suddenly felt very far away.

Hero tucked his head under Ben's hand. The feeling of the dog's warm fur brought Ben back to himself.

Ben couldn't see who was inside the car—was it the chief? The mayor?

At last, the car doors swung open at exactly the same time. Two police officers climbed out, their faces blank, betraying nothing. One of them was Officer Perillo, who worked in the K-9 unit with Ben's dad. She had helped show Ben how to train Hero—and

Hero had been Perillo's canine teacher when she first joined the unit.

In fact, Perillo was one of the officers who had arrested Mitch, the head of the dogfighting ring, after Ben and Hero had found him.

Ben's mom rushed out to the driveway and stopped by his side. She clasped her hands together in front of her chin, holding her breath.

"Is my dad missing? Is he okay?" Ben's throat was dry, and his heart was about to burst from his chest. He took a step forward and tried to read Officer Perillo's face. She looked right at him, her eyes filled with concern and kindness.

"Don't worry, Ben," Perillo said. "It's going to be okay."

Did that mean his dad was all right?

Ben's mom reached out and put her hand on his arm. Hero stepped forward, positioning himself between the officers and Ben.

"Mommy! Benny!" Erin called from the doorway, where she stood with a frightened look on her face. "Is that Daddy?"

"I got her," Noah and Jack said at the same time. They jogged over and led Erin into the house.

Ben's mom gripped his arm tightly. She took a breath. "Is he missing? Do the convicts have him?" she asked, her voice steady.

"We don't know," Perillo said. "But we haven't heard from him since last night."

Ben felt his mom sway a little. He put an arm around her shoulder to steady her.

"He was supposed to check in every hour," Perillo went on. "When was the last time you talked to him?"

"He texted around midnight," Ben's mom said. "He said everything was fine and that he felt like he and Scout were getting close to the convicts."

Perillo shot a look at the other officer, who walked a few feet away and started talking into the walkie-talkie clipped to his shoulder.

"That's good," Perillo said. "That's almost an hour after we last heard from him. That means another hour that everything was fine." Perillo stepped closer and took Ben's mom's hand. "Listen, Jessica, everything's going to be okay. Dave is the best cop out there. He knows how to take care of himself."

"Thanks, Janine." Ben's mom managed a weak smile. "I know. And he has Scout with him too."

Perillo nodded. "Scout is smart and strong—like

this guy right here." She reached down and scratched Hero behind the ears. "Scout is going to look out for the Sarge the same way Hero would." Perillo turned to Ben. "We have every officer on the force, plus federal agents, out there looking for him. We're going to find him."

Ben nodded and bit his bottom lip to steady it. "Okay," he muttered. Hero looked up at the sound of his voice. Ben ran his fingers over his dog's smooth forehead.

"Remember all the things Hero did to keep you safe?"

Ben nodded.

"That's what Scout is going to do for your dad. He has your dad's back—you know that, right?"

"Yeah, I know. Thanks." Ben thought of something. "Officer Perillo?"

"Yes?"

"What were they in for? The guys who escaped, I mean?"

Perillo sighed. She looked to Ben's mom, who nodded.

"Armed robbery," Perillo said.

Ben felt queasy.

"I know you're scared, Ben, but we got this," Perillo reassured him. "I need you to do something for me, though."

Ben took a couple of quick breaths and got it together. "Sure."

"I need you to stay here with your mom and sister. Can you do that?"

"No," Ben blurted out before he could stop himself. His mom spun around to look at him, and Perillo's eyes went wide. A wave of frustration and adrenaline washed over him. "I want to help—I want to go look for my dad! You guys know Hero and I can find him!"

"Ben—" Perillo started.

"Ben," his mom said, putting her hands on Ben's shoulders. She tipped his chin up and locked eyes with him. "We need you. Erin and I need you here."

"Dad needs me more!" Ben cried.

"Ben, please. Listen to me," His mom's voice cracked, and she pulled him into a tight hug. "It's going to be okay."

Ben could feel his mom's heart beating through her chest. She was as scared as he was.

5

BEN'S MIND SPUN IN AN ENDLESS LOOP.

Was his dad safe? Was he hurt?

Jack and Noah had gone home and kept texting to see if there had been any news. Ben just kept replying with one word: *Nope.* His friends had offered to hang out at his house, but Ben just needed to be alone.

He wandered the house. Hero followed him from room to room, his head and tail hanging low. He wasn't going to let Ben be alone for a split second.

"I know, buddy," Ben said to Hero as they sat together on Ben's bed. "I don't want to be stuck here any more than you do. But we don't have a choice. We promised."

Hero looked up at Ben with big, sad eyes. The soft fur of his forehead was wrinkled with worry. He whimpered and dropped his head into Ben's lap.

Ben didn't know how Hero could tell that things weren't okay—but he could. He *felt* that Ben was upset.

"What should we do?" Ben asked Hero.

Hero looked up at him without lifting his head. He let out a short, sharp snort.

Ben studied his dog's sleek dark face and scratched the soft spot around Hero's whiskers.

One of the things Ben loved most about Hero was how calm and solid he was—how strong. He always knew what to do. Sometimes Ben envied Hero's clear sense of purpose, his lack of self-doubt. If someone he loved was in danger, Hero acted. He never worried about his own safety or whether or not it was the "right" choice. He just did what his instinct and training told him to do: help.

Ben watched Hero for another moment.

This time Ben knew what he needed to do.

"Come on, boy," Ben said. Hero was on his feet so fast it was almost as if he'd never been lying down. He stood by the door, his head up, his senses alert. His ears twitched as he listened to the sounds of the house

31

and the street beyond it. He watched as Ben laced up his sneakers and pulled on a sweatshirt.

"Come, Hero. We need a few things." Hero followed Ben down the hall to his parents' room and stood guard while Ben rummaged through his dad's closet. Ben emerged with his dad's worn-out police academy sweatshirt, which he wrapped tightly around his own waist, knotting it in front.

They headed downstairs.

Ben's mom had drifted off to sleep on the couch, with Erin curled up next to her. Ben stood in the doorway for a long moment, watching them. Then he scribbled a quick note and left it on the kitchen counter.

He knew his mom would be mad when she woke up and discovered Ben was gone.

At the same time, he didn't feel he had a choice.

He had to act.

Ben opened the front door and slipped outside, Hero by his side. He couldn't stay trapped in his house, waiting for the phone to ring, while the best search dog in Mississippi was leaning against his leg.

Ben's phone dinged in his pocket. It was a group text from Jack to him and Noah.

What's the word? Jack wrote. *I'm coming over after dinner, like it or not.*

Me too, Noah wrote.

Ben took one last look at his house, then turned back to his phone.

Don't bother, he wrote. *I'm coming to you. Meet at Jack's in 15.*

Ben pedaled fast.

Hero ran at his side, wearing a black vest with the words K-9 UNIT written across it in neon yellow letters. His movements were fluid, purposeful—graceful. As hard as Ben was pedaling, Hero looked like he was barely breaking a sweat.

Noah and Jack stood waiting for them on Jack's lawn, worried looks on their faces.

"Is everything okay?" Noah asked.

"Did you hear something about your dad?" Jack asked.

Ben shook his head. He hopped off his bike and

let it fall to the ground. He pulled his backpack off his shoulders and tossed it down on the grass.

"We haven't heard anything," he said. "But I need your help."

Noah looked down at Ben's backpack, then at Hero in his K-9 vest. Ben saw the wheels turning in his best friend's head.

"You and Hero are going to look for your dad." Noah wasn't asking a question—he was making a statement.

"Yeah."

Jack looked from Ben to Noah and back again. "What do you need us to do?"

"I need supplies. Snacks, water, walkie-talkies."

Without a word, Noah and Jack turned and headed inside. Jack's mom was at the hospital where she worked as a doctor, and they had the house to themselves. The three boys filled up Ben's backpack with energy bars and water, maps and phone chargers, fifteen dollars in cash and a familiar-looking compass. They hadn't been able to use their phones when they'd gotten stranded in the woods during the hurricane; that compass had come in handy.

The backpack was stuffed to the limit, and the

zipper barely stayed closed. Ben hefted the bag onto his shoulders.

Noah and Jack looked at each other, then at Ben.

"We're coming with you," Jack said.

"You can't stop us," Noah added.

Ben sighed. He should have known his friends weren't going to want him to go looking for his dad alone. They had been with him and Hero through plenty of adventures.

But this time was different.

"Thanks, guys," Ben said. "That's really cool of you."

"I sense a major 'but' coming," Jack said drily.

"I sense a major 'I gotta do this on my own' coming," Noah said, rolling his eyes.

"Ha," Ben shot back. "But no. First of all, Noah—you're not exactly in the best shape."

Noah looked down at his injured arm and shrugged, then screwed up his face in pain. "True," he said.

"And I need someone to look out for Erin and my mom. Someone has to be there if they hear bad n—" Ben couldn't finish the sentence, because he couldn't even finish the thought. "I need you guys to be my home base, okay?"

Noah looked down at the floor. Jack looked up at the ceiling.

Ben understood. He wouldn't want to let either one of them go off by himself either.

"Fine," Noah said.

"Okay," Jack said.

The boys walked single file into the front yard, where Ben's bike lay waiting. They stood silently on the lawn for a moment. No one knew what to say.

"Thanks, guys."

Ben adjusted the heavy backpack and got on his bike. Hero stood right next to him, his head cocked to the side, his eyes locked on Ben.

Hero was waiting for his signal.

Ben untied his dad's sweatshirt from around his waist. He held it out for Hero to sniff.

Hero ran his snout over the soft, faded fabric. He paused at the frayed neckline and gave it an extra sniff. He exhaled sharply to clear his nose, then sniffed some more.

"Hero!" Ben said, his voice full of urgency: "Find Dad!"

Hero took off like a shot. With one last look back at his friends, Ben followed. Hero flew ahead so fast that Ben had to stand up on his bike and pedal hard to keep up.

The late afternoon sun was low in the sky as they reached the end of the block. Without pausing to let Ben catch up, Hero turned right at the corner, his muscles rippling and his gorgeous black coat glistening.

Ben followed as closely as he could. Hero never slowed his pace. He was on a mission, and time and speed were of the essence.

For a mile or more, they headed down quiet residential streets. The only sound was the whirring of Ben's bike tires on the asphalt. No one was out in their front yards or wandering the sidewalks, but Ben saw flashes of life through the windows of the houses he rode by. It seemed like every television played the evening news—updating the townspeople about his missing father.

Soon, they turned onto a road that led through the more industrial end of town, where businesses and warehouses had closed for the day.

Ben recognized this road, and he realized where Hero was leading him. His heart—already pounding from the hard bike riding—beat even faster.

Hero was leading him straight for the woods.

Ben had been tromping around in these woods his whole life. When he wasn't at baseball practice, he and Hero played ball and wandered around there every day after school. This was where they had found Scout, when he was just a tiny, scruffy pup who hadn't eaten in days.

And Ben and Hero had gotten trapped in these woods with Noah, Jack, and Scout during the hurricane. They had rescued Scout from an alligator, found a Boy Scout troop, and played an epic game of baseball.

But most important, these were the same woods where the two escaped convicts could easily be hiding at that very moment—with Ben's dad.

Ben swallowed hard. This wasn't going to be easy. If he and Hero found his dad, that meant they'd probably find the convicts too. And then what?

It was growing dark. He had a flashlight, but if they were trying to sneak up on two criminals, then the last thing he should do was use it. That meant Ben would have to follow Hero in complete darkness as evening turned into night, with only the neon lettering on Hero's vest to guide him. And Ben would have to communicate with Hero without making any sound.

Ben was going to have to be on his guard—and put his faith entirely in Hero.

Hero would hear and assess every snap of a twig, every rustle of a leaf that sounded out of the ordinary. Hero would sniff the air carefully, repeatedly, and sense even the faintest hint of a person among the trees. Hero could smell someone from miles away. And . . . well, if it came down to it, Hero was pretty great at attacking bad guys too.

Hero dipped through the tree line and into the woods. The leaves overhead blocked out what little sunlight remained, and the air was chilly and damp. Despite the sweat he had worked up riding his bike, Ben shivered.

Hero snuffled at the ground as he ran, then raised his head and sniffed at the air. He swiveled his head back and forth, taking in thousands of different smells at once, sorting them, then picking the right one to follow.

They stuck to the edge of the woods, never going deeper than a couple hundred feet from the tree line. Ben was confused—why would the men who had taken his dad stay on the perimeter of the woods, where they would be more likely to be spotted? Why wouldn't they head for cover deeper into the forest?

But he trusted Hero. There was no better

search-and-rescue dog out there. If Hero said this was the way they needed to go, then this was where they were going.

After a mile or so of hard riding, Hero took a sharp left and zipped out of the woods. Ben followed him off the dirt and onto a paved road.

Ben knew exactly where they were. They rode for another quarter mile before Hero stopped and sat down, his signal that he had found what he was supposed to be looking for.

Ben shook his head in amazement.

"Hero, you're one smart dog," he said, catching his breath and laughing.

Hero stared at the wide, squat building across the road.

It was the Gulfport Police Station.

6

BEN HELD OPEN THE FRONT DOOR of the station for Hero, who sauntered into the building like nothing had changed—like he was still a police dog on the force and he was reporting for duty.

Hero walked right past the officer seated at the front desk. The tall, burly man leaped out of his seat—which looked tiny underneath him—and ran around the desk. He made a beeline for Hero with his arms open wide.

"Hero!" the officer cried, dropping to his knees and embracing the dog. "I've missed you, buddy."

Hero sniffed at the collar of the man's uniform. "You're sniffing for the Sarge, aren't you, pal?" The man's eyes softened. He put his big, meaty hands on either side of Hero's head and scratched him behind the ears. "If anyone can find him, it's you."

The policeman stood up, walked over to Ben, and enveloped him in a massive bear hug, squeezing the air out of Ben's lungs.

"Hey, Ben."

"Hey, Officer Biagini," Ben grunted into the man's chest. Officer Biagini released Ben, who inhaled gratefully. "Your dad's going to be all right, okay?"

"Okay." Ben smiled weakly.

"Did they ask you to come in?" Officer Biagini asked as he led Ben and Hero down the hall. Usually the station was busy with activity, but today it was weirdly quiet. Ben didn't know if that was a good thing or a bad thing. "To help out, I mean?"

"Um, not exactly," Ben said.

"Ah, I see." Officer Biagini smiled down at Ben. "Well, I'm sure they'll be glad to see you."

They stopped at the end of a long hallway. In front of them was a gigantic rectangular room, filled to the brim with a sea of desks.

Now Ben knew why the rest of the station was so quiet: *Everyone* was in here. A huge group of officers hustled around the room, talking with one another, tapping at their computers, speaking into their phones and walkie-talkies, and gesturing wildly over the desks. Phones dinged and rang and bleeped. A TV hung high on the wall, with the local news playing on mute. Ben saw his dad's name, Officer David Landry, run across the bottom of the screen.

There had been a few other times when Ben had seen the whole force working together on a big case like this—but usually his dad was at the center of the action. He'd never thought that his dad would *be* the case.

At the center of the busy mass of policewomen and -men stood the head of the force, Chief Roberts. He was barking out orders, answering questions, squinting at his cell phone, and signing forms.

"Ben! Hero!" Officer Perillo's voice called out over the hubbub. She ran over to Ben. "What are you doing here?"

The room went silent. Officers froze mid-sentence. All heads turned toward Ben and Hero. Even the chief looked up from his phone and locked eyes with Ben.

Ben broke out in a cold sweat.

"Uh, hi?"

Chief Roberts broke the awkward silence.

"Hello, son," he said to Ben. "It's good to see you. We're doing everything we can to find your father." The chief's phone vibrated in his hand. "Excuse me, Ben," he said. He raised the phone to his ear. "Yeah. What do you have for me?" He turned away and bowed his head as he listened carefully to the person on the other end.

Officer Perillo put one arm around Ben's shoulder and reached down with the other to pet the top of Hero's head. Hero nuzzled her palm and licked her fingers. One by one, the other officers returned to their work.

"Ben—what is it?" Perillo asked. "Did you hear from your father?"

"No—I just—" Ben surveyed all the people who were working so hard to find his dad. For a second, his resolve wavered. He knew these were the best and smartest law enforcement officers in the entire state— and he was lucky they were on the case. How could a thirteen-year-old kid possibly help?

But that question didn't change what he knew in his gut.

"Hero and I can help."

"Ben—"

"We can find my dad. You know we can. You know no one is better trained than Hero—" Ben waved a hand toward his dog, who sat with his front legs perfectly aligned, looking up at them with rounded eyes. Hero flicked his ears at the urgent sound in Ben's voice.

Hero was ready. He just needed Ben's command.

"Ben," Perillo began, her tone apologetic. Ben hated when grown-ups used that I'm-talking-to-a-kid voice. "You're right. No one is better than Hero. And you're darned good at tracking yourself. But this is a really dangerous situation."

"We can handle it," Ben said. His moment of self-doubt was gone. "Hero and I have done this before."

"I know," Perillo said. "But—"

"We got something!" Chief Roberts cried out from across the room. "Everyone, let's huddle."

Perillo shot Ben a worried look.

"Ben," she said gently. "You and Hero should go wait in the lobby. I'll be out in a minute."

Ben understood what Perillo was trying to tell him. If it was bad news, she didn't want him to hear it this way, in front of all these people. "Thanks, but it's

45

okay." He swallowed the lump in his throat and braced himself.

Perillo stared at him for a long moment, her hand gripping his shoulder tightly. She exhaled. "Okay."

Perillo, Ben, and Hero joined the group that had gathered in a half circle at the center of the room. Perillo nodded at the chief, telling him to continue.

Chief Roberts pressed his lips tightly together, pausing for a moment to weigh his words carefully.

"We got a lead," the chief said.

Ben's heart clenched like a fist. He gasped with relief. The officers let out a collective cheer.

"Sergeant Landry's cell phone pinged a tower on the northern end of the national forest. But then it stopped."

"How long ago, boss?" one of the officers asked.

"Eighteen hundred hours." Roberts looked at his watch. "That's . . . less than twenty minutes ago. We need to follow this fast, but bear in mind—it could mean nothing. Maybe his phone isn't even with him anymore. We don't know. We can't let hope get in the way of our judgment here, people." The officers looked down at the floor, letting the chief's words of caution sink in. "Be smart, and be careful. Now let's move."

Ben ran the chief's words through his head again, scanning them for clues. Why would his dad's phone only send a signal for a moment? If his phone was working, why didn't he make a phone call or send a text?

Ben grabbed Perillo's arm. "He turned his phone on then turned it off again. That's what that means, right?"

Her eyes grew wide with recognition as she grasped what he was saying.

"He did it on purpose," Ben went on. "He wasn't able to use the phone. So he was . . ." His mind was racing. "He was sending us a signal."

"I think so," Perillo said.

Ben was filled with nervous energy. He ran a hand through his hair and turned away from Perillo, took a few steps, then turned back. Hero whimpered at him, and Ben reflexively wrapped his fingers around his dog's collar. "If he had to turn his phone back off, that means . . ."

Perillo nodded, her expression grim. "That means he's not alone, Ben. They've got him."

The convicts.

Ben's dad had been captured. A wave of fear

crashed over Ben. Images flooded his brain: His dad being taken. His dad fighting back. His dad tied up.

Ben's chest was tight with a fear that bordered on panic. *Breathe, Ben,* he heard his father say. *Take one step at a time.*

Ben forced himself to exhale slowly and take a deep breath in. The knot in his stomach began to loosen. He began to think more clearly. And as he did, his fear crystallized into something else: determination.

If his dad was out there with those two criminals, then Ben most definitely wasn't going to sit around here waiting for someone else to go and save him.

"Please," Ben said, his voice filled with desperation. "If they have him, then we have to hurry. We have to find him. No one can do it faster than Hero. We both know that."

Perillo squeezed her eyes shut as she considered what he was saying. Ben waited. Finally she looked right at him. "Wait here." She walked briskly to the chief and spoke into his ear. The chief leaned in to listen, looking up at Ben as Perillo spoke. Perillo gestured toward Ben and Hero. Chief Roberts put a hand to his forehead and shook his head.

Perillo stood back, crossed her arms, and waited.

The chief seemed to be weighing something. Finally, after another shake of his head, he nodded.

Perillo turned on her heels and crossed the room quickly back to Ben.

"You're coming with me," she said, pulling him by the arm.

"What do you mean? I'm not leaving!"

"Nope. You're not leaving. *We're* leaving. We need to get you suited up. I have to find some gear that fits you. Looks like Hero's all set."

"Wait—what do you mean?" Ben was confused. He wasn't being sent home?

Perillo was walking fast. Ben scrambled to keep up. "You can't be on my rescue squad if you're not wearing something I can see in the dark."

Ben couldn't believe his ears. "He said Hero and I can come?"

"Yep."

"What did you tell him?"

She stopped midstride and turned to face Ben. "The truth. I told him that Hero is our best bet of finding your dad fast. And that you come with the dog. You're the one Hero listens to. Hero knows your dad, and you know Hero. We need you. Both."

"Thank you—I can't even believe . . ." Ben trailed off. "What did the chief say?"

"He said there's only one condition."

Ben's heart sank. "What?"

"Don't mess up."

7

BEN HEARD THE BEATING OF THE helicopter blades
through his headphones. He gripped the armrest and
watched the ground move farther away as the copter
rose into the air. Hero sat calmly beside him, unfazed
by the loud noise and the extreme heights.

Hero had ridden in a helicopter many times when
he'd been on the job with Ben's dad. Ben, however,
had only flown in one once before, when he and Hero
were rescued from the woods after the hurricane. But
he had barely noticed the flight that time. This time he
was aware that it was a lot less like flying in a plane—
and a lot more like riding a roller coaster—than he

had expected. His stomach swooped and rolled as the aircraft tilted to head north, rising as it went.

Ben's dad's cell phone had pinged at the far northern end of the woods—the same woods where Ben and Hero had spent so much time together.

Ben surveyed the land below. What if his dad was down there somewhere? What if they were flying over him right that second?

Ben pushed the worry out of his mind. They were on their way and they were doing the best they could do. He looked over at Perillo. She was staring at a tablet in her hand, reviewing communications with the rest of the search team and a map of where she and Ben were headed.

She gave him a thumbs-up and spoke into the microphone attached to her headset. Her voice came through Ben's headphones. "We'll be there in just a few minutes. We're landing a couple of miles from the site. Then we have to hike in. You good?"

Ben nodded in reply and turned back to the window. His stomach was getting used to the motion of the helicopter, and he started to relax.

Hero scooted over and rested his muzzle on the window, his wet nose pressed against the glass. They sat like that for the rest of the flight, Ben's hand on Hero's neck. He ran his fingers through Hero's silky fur.

As he often did, Ben wondered what Hero was thinking at that moment. There was no way Hero understood the details of what was happening—that Ben's dad had been taken by two escaped convicts who were probably armed and definitely dangerous. But Ben had no doubt that Hero understood, on some level, that Sergeant Landry was in trouble. Hero knew that Ben's dad needed him—that the whole family needed him. All of Hero's training and all of the powerful instincts he had honed over the years made him amazingly attuned not just to smells and sights and sounds, but to emotions too.

The helicopter hovered over a wide clearing near the edge of the national forest. Stretching out ahead of them as far as Ben could see was a blanket of thick foliage and dense treetops.

"I'm going to put her down now," the pilot said into the communication system. "Hang on."

Ben's stomach flipped as the helicopter moved rapidly downward, but the landing was smoother than he'd expected. They dropped right into the middle of the clearing and touched down gently.

Perillo unbuckled herself quickly while Ben fumbled with the straps. He jogged out of the helicopter after her. Hero bounded out ahead of them both and ran in a wide circle, sniffing at the ground. His movements were quick and jumpy—almost frantic. He picked his head up to listen and sniff at the air, then dropped his nose back down again. He skittered a few steps in one direction, then another.

Dirt flew up in little puffs around his paws as the helicopter blades churned behind them.

Ben had never seen Hero like this before. Like he always did, Hero was tracking and cataloging the thousands of scents he was picking up, but there was something else going on too. Ben watched as Hero's ears went up and his head swung around toward one sound, then another. He saw Hero's muzzle twitch and his eyes cast about, unable to rest on one sight. Ben crouched down.

"Hero, come!" Ben said.

Hero's ears flicked back on his head, but he didn't follow the command immediately, like he always did. Instead, he hesitated—so quickly it was almost imperceptible. But Ben felt it.

"Hero, come!" Ben repeated. Hero trotted over

reluctantly. As he neared, Ben heard him softly whining.

Ben wasn't sure at first what was happening. He wrapped his arms around Hero's neck, but instead of leaning into Ben as usual, Hero tried to pull away.

That's when Ben understood. His highly trained, levelheaded, lifesaving dog was *upset*.

Ben let him go, and Hero zigzagged across the clearing again, tracking Ben's dad's trail as anxiously as before.

"Officer Perillo," Ben called out over the chugging of the propeller and the whir of the engine behind them. "Do you see what I'm seeing?"

"Yeah," she shouted back. "That's not like him." They watched Hero in silence for a moment. "I think he really wants to find your dad."

"That makes two of us."

"Three." Perillo turned to Ben. He saw a look in her eye that he recognized: It was the steely resolve and laser focus of a cop about to embark on a dangerous mission. "We need to get going. You ready, Ben?"

"I'm ready."

Before Ben had the chance to give Hero the search command, Hero rocketed across the clearing, toward the tree line on the eastern edge. When he got a few feet from the dark forest, he looked back at Ben, barked once, and sat down.

Hero had picked up a scent.

"Let's go!" Perillo jogged toward the dog.

"Good boy," Ben called, following close behind Perillo. He gave Hero a dog treat from his pocket. "Now, Hero—*go!*"

Hero bolted into the trees so fast Ben thought his eyes were playing tricks on him. The darkness swallowed the black dog. If it weren't for the neon yellow letters on Hero's vest, Ben never would have been able to see him as he moved deeper into the woods.

Ben and Perillo ran to keep up, the light from their flashlights bouncing up and down as they moved. They hopped over roots and skirted rocks that littered their path. As the sound of the helicopter faded away behind them, Hero became a speck in the distance ahead.

Hero picked up speed. He ran off the trail and headed deeper and deeper into the woods, without pausing, for a mile, then two miles. Ben thought the dog would collapse from exhaustion.

But Hero just kept going. He had latched on to the

scent of Ben's dad, and he wasn't going to stop until he found him.

Perillo slowed down a few yards ahead of Ben. She bent forward and put her hands on her knees, catching her breath.

Ben caught up to her, and she put a hand on his shoulder.

"He needs you, Ben," she said between breaths.

"What do you mean?" Ben was panting. This was as much running as he did in an entire baseball practice—plus a few extra sprints.

"Hero's tracking, but can you see a difference in how he's behaving?"

Ben nodded. "Yeah. It's like he's . . . I don't know . . . a little wild or something."

"Let me ask you this, Ben—why did Hero rescue all those people over the years?"

Ben ran through the list of people he knew Hero had saved—everyone from old ladies to babies to an entire Boy Scout troop. Hero never wavered in his determination to find each and every one of those people. But he also had no reason—other than training and instinct—to find them.

"Because that's what he does."

"Right," Perillo said. "He did it because he's a search-and-rescue dog. But it's different this time. Why do you think he's trying to find your dad?"

The answer was easy. "Because he loves him." Ben was starting to see what Perillo was getting at.

"That's right. He loves your dad the way you do. It's the same way Hero loves you. How did you feel when Hero was in trouble?"

Ben shuddered at the memory. In his mind, he replayed the horrible scene of Hero getting attacked by two vicious dogs at the dogfighting ring. "Pretty awful."

"And did you do things you would normally do? Or did you act differently?"

"I acted differently."

"So Hero feels the same way right now. You know he would do literally anything for you or your dad, right?"

"Yeah, and I'd do anything for him." Ben squinted into the darkness to find Hero. He saw a tiny neon streak about thirty yards ahead. "So he's tracking differently?"

"Yes. He senses that your dad's in danger, so he's

feeling a kind of urgency that's more than just the tracking instinct—or his training."

A shot of hope flashed through Ben. "Does that mean he'll find my dad faster?"

"Well . . . not exactly." Perillo straightened up and shook out her arms and legs. She started walking quickly after Hero. Ben had to take two steps for every one of hers to keep up. "It can actually slow him down. It can mean that he's stressed, which can make him distracted."

It had never occurred to Ben that Hero could be anything but perfect.

In Ben's mind, Hero never failed, never faltered, and never slowed down, even if he was hurt. He couldn't bear the thought that Hero could be sad—it sent a pang through Ben's chest that made him feel even worse.

"He's a good dog. He'll be okay—he just needs our support," Perillo said, as if she knew what Ben was thinking.

"How do we do that?" Ben asked. The neon speck was getting smaller. They needed to hurry or they might lose him.

"You need to take over."

"What do you mean?" Ben asked.

"I mean that you need to be his boss—more so than ever before. He needs you to lead him."

"Like, be the alpha dog?"

"Exactly. You need to be the alpha. You two are a team, but every team needs a leader. And that's you." Perillo pointed a finger at Ben's chest.

"So what do I do?"

"Well, first things first—you need to stop him right now. He's too far away."

Ben figured that wasn't so hard. "Hero!" he called ahead, his voice echoing in the quiet woods. "Stop."

Hero kept running.

"Hero!" Ben couldn't keep a note of surprise out of his voice. It wasn't like his dog to ignore Ben's command. "HERO!" Ben's voice was getting higher as well as louder.

Hero kept running.

Ben looked at Perillo, unsure what to do next.

"Use your voice," she said simply. "Dig deep, Ben."

He filled his lungs with air and, when he called out Hero's name again, projected his voice far out across the woods.

"HERO! STOP!" Ben's voice vibrated deep within his chest. It sounded stronger and richer than usual.

Hero stopped. The neon flicker of his vest went still, then grew bigger as Ben and Perillo approached him.

"That was good, Ben," Perillo said. When they were within a few feet of Hero, the dog started moving again—but he was walking instead of running this time. Perillo tipped her head in Hero's direction. "See? He still has other ideas."

Ben shook his head. This was truly unlike Hero.

"There will be times when you can't communicate with him verbally," Perillo went on. "So what would you do then?"

"Use hand commands?" Ben wasn't sure how that would work in the woods, in the dark.

"Well," Perillo replied, "yes, but a hand command won't always work. He wouldn't be able to see one right now, for example. And soon we're going to be closing in on these guys, and we're not going to want to shout and tip them off that we're coming. So what would you do if you couldn't call out to him?"

Ben had no idea. "Um . . ."

"You'd have to rely on some kind of sound, but

more than that—you'd have to rely on how he hears the sound coming from you."

"I don't understand," Ben said.

"It's kind of hard to talk about—it's a lot easier to do. Try something for me, would you?"

Ben nodded.

"Make a sound like this." Perillo made a loud clucking sound with her mouth.

Ben did the same. Hero's ears flickered slightly, but he didn't so much as slow down.

"He didn't really care about that, did he?"

"No." Ben shook his head.

"Right," Perillo said. "So try it again—but this time do it in a way that you know he'll hear and understand."

Ben thought about her instructions for a moment. He couldn't exactly explain it, but he got what she meant.

"Tsk tsk!" He made the sound again, this time a little more forcefully. Hero's ears pricked up and he tilted his head to the side.

"Again," Perillo instructed Ben. "You got his attention, but this time, you're in charge. Think about what you want him to do."

"*TSK TSK!*" The sound was firmer, sharper-edged. Hero's ears went up again, and he paused mid-step, turning back to look at Ben. He watched Ben for a moment, then turned his head forward and began walking and sniffing at the ground once more.

"Nice," Perillo said. "You got through to him. But now you need him to stop—and stay stopped. Again."

Ben took a couple of breaths and cleared his throat. He watched Hero's sleek black fur and muscular back, and his tail pointed straight back and curled up at the end.

"You're talking directly to him," Perillo said. "It's just the two of you. You speak your own language."

Ben rounded his lips, put his tongue to the roof of his mouth, and made the same noise again, but this time it was firm, and loud, and quick. It wasn't just a sound, it was a *command.*

Hero stopped.

Ben and Perillo were about ten feet away. Ben made the sound again, but a little faster—building on what he had just communicated to his dog—and this time, Hero sat down. He looked over his shoulder at Ben, his dark brown eyes big and round. Gone were the frantic movements and rapid pace. Hero looked calmer, more focused—and ready to do what Ben needed him to do, instead of what Hero *wanted* to do.

"Good boy."

Hero watched Ben approach.

Ben reached his dog's side and squatted down next to him, scratching Hero's back. "Good boy," he repeated. Ben gave Hero a treat from his pocket and tipped his water bottle to Hero's mouth. Hero snapped up the food and water, then resumed his still position, waiting for a command, his eyes on Ben.

Ben didn't know how else to describe it: Hero looked relieved. He *needed* Ben to take charge.

"What now, Ben?" Perillo asked.

Ben thought for a moment. "He needs to stay closer. We don't know who's out there, so I don't want him to get too far ahead of us."

"Right. So, tell him."

Ben took a deep breath and stood up. He looked down at Hero and held his gaze. Hero was ready to go but didn't so much as flex a muscle. He was hanging on Ben's every word.

"Hero," Ben said, his voice clear and firm. "Stay close. *Find Dad!*"

Hero leaped to his feet and shot a few feet ahead of

Ben and Perillo. He grazed the ground with his snout, moving it back and forth, then raising it to sniff at the air. He trotted at a steady clip. When he started to get a few yards farther out, Ben repeated himself. "Hero, stay close!"

Hero slowed his pace without looking up. He forged ahead, never moving out of their sight.

"Atta boy," Ben said.

8

"THAT WAS AMAZING, BEN," PERILLO SAID. "I'm proud of you." They trudged ahead side by side. Her words floated to him across the darkness.

"Thanks." He shrugged.

"You know," Perillo went on, "we really come to think of our dogs as our partners—our equals. And in so many ways they are. But that's the way we see it, not the way they see it. They see us as the boss, and that's the way it should be."

They were quiet for a moment. Ben listened to the underbrush crunching under their feet as they walked behind Hero.

"It took me a while to feel that way with my first

K-9 partner," Perillo said. "Moose was such a sweetheart. And tough too. Like a warrior. It was about a year before I really felt like we had it down, you know? Like I could get through to her no matter what was happening." Perillo laughed. "But you know what? She had one strange fear that I could never get her past."

"What was it?"

"For the life of her, she couldn't jump through a car window—"

"Wait," Ben interrupted, "dogs can do that? Jump through a car window?"

"Sure they can."

"When the car's moving?"

"When the car's moving."

"No way."

"Pretty amazing, right? Anyway, Moose just couldn't do it. She could climb ladders, track while swimming—I mean, she was incredible. Second only to Hero. But any time I commanded her to jump into a car, she froze. It was really frustrating. And it was keeping her from going out on the job."

"Wow. So what did you do?"

"Well, your dad taught me what I just taught you, and it worked."

The mere mention of his dad brought a swell of love—and fear—into Ben's heart.

He had heard so many stories about his dad from other cops and from people in town over the years—funny tales, expressions of gratitude, moments of total awe—but this time it was different.

This time, he didn't know if he would ever see his dad again.

Ben and Perillo fell silent as Hero tracked a path in front of them. He stayed close. They were deep into the woods now. The quiet around them deepened, and the foliage grew denser. Something in the air began to feel different.

Hero slowed to a stop. He sniffed heavily at one spot, then moved a few steps, stopped, and focused on a new spot.

"What is it, Hero?" Ben whispered.

Hero looked up at Ben, then turned back to his work. He moved farther ahead, then a little farther, finally leading them into a small clearing. Every few sniffs, Hero snorted sharply to clear his nostrils. His muzzle and whiskers twitched as he worked.

Ben smelled the familiar scent of campfire smoke. It was faint.

Hero began to walk—and sniff—in a large circle. Ben stepped closer to see.

"Officer Perillo!" Ben whispered. "Over here."

She rushed to his side. They stood together looking down at a flattened, burned circle in the underbrush.

At the center of it, a small bed of orange embers flickered and darkened just before going out. They were barely lit—but they had definitely been burning hot not long ago.

Someone had just put out a fire.

Someone who might have heard them coming.

Someone who could still be close by.

"Stay close, Ben," Perillo whispered. With one arm, she pushed him behind her and began to turn in a slow circle, scanning the area carefully.

Ben held his breath. Hero was a few feet away. Ben whistled—so softly it was almost no more than an exhale—to get his attention, then, when Hero was looking at him, Ben gave him the hand signal for *come*. Hero snapped to Ben's side and sat down next to his leg. Ben gave him the hand signal for *stay*. The dog eyed the trees around them, his ears up and back.

The three of them stood silently, listening, watching, waiting.

Nothing.

Perillo released her grip on Ben's arm but remained alert. Hero dropped his head to the ground and began sniffing again.

"Okay, Hero," Ben said. Hero stood up and began to move around.

"They can't be far," Perillo whispered to Ben. "We need backup." She pulled her walkie-talkie from its clip on her shoulder and spoke softly into it.

As Ben watched Hero follow a scent around the edge of the clearing, his eyes fell on a large rock resting by the base of a tree. Something just beneath it looked out of place. Ben got closer and spotted a shiny red object jutting out from under the rock, half covered in dirt and leaves.

Ben leaned down to investigate.

It was an empty packet of Big Red gum.

He picked it up, and his fingers brushed against a large leaf lying on the ground. The leaf moved to reveal a small triangle of fabric, frayed at the edges as if it had been ripped from a larger piece. It was covered in dirt, but its bright orange color was still clear.

Like an orange prison jumpsuit.

Like the color an escaped convict would wear.

Ben's heart pounded as the reality sank in: If the prisoners had just been here, then his dad had to be nearby.

He started to turn toward Perillo to tell her what he had found. As he did, he saw something sparkly out of the corner of his eye, just underneath the rock. Was it another clue?

Ben had spent his whole life wandering through the woods of Gulfport. He had camped out more times than he could remember. He knew the rules of safety and common sense that guided anyone who ventured into the woods.

But in his excitement he forgot everything.

Ben reached out a hand and, with shaking fingers, lifted the rock.

As he did, he realized two things at exactly the same instant: Hero was suddenly at his side and going nuts, barking and snarling and baring his teeth; and something was moving under the rock.

Ben turned to shush Hero—and at just that moment, the sparkly thing under the rock shot out toward him.

Before he had time to process what it was, Ben felt a sharp sting, burning, and warmth spreading up his arm.

That's when he saw two small, bloody puncture wounds on his wrist, and he understood instantly what had just happened.

Ben had been bitten by a snake.

9

BEN STAGGERED BACKWARD AND FELL TO the ground. His arm was on fire, and he was so woozy he couldn't even lift his head. He tried to call out Perillo's name, but no sound came out. He let his head rest on the ground and stared up at the leaves on the tops of the trees, far above him, swaying and revealing flashes of the night sky.

His eyelids grew heavier and heavier.

Just as he was about to lose consciousness, Ben felt pressure and warmth on his chest.

It was Hero.

His dog was nudging and pawing at him, licking his neck. Hero barked to alert Perillo, and the sound echoed through Ben's brain in slow waves, like he was hearing it from miles away.

"Ben!" Perillo cried out in alarm.

She ran to his side as Hero began licking the wound on Ben's wrist. His coarse tongue hurt Ben's ruptured skin—the pain was unlike anything Ben had ever felt—but somehow, through his hazy thoughts, Ben understood that Hero was trying to draw the snake venom from his body.

Ben tried to speak again. He formed the words in his mouth—*Thanks, Hero*—but all that came out was a hoarse whisper.

Perillo knelt down and put her hands on either side of his face. "Look at me, Ben," she said loudly and firmly. Her voice pierced the fog and pain that had overcome him. He tried to look at her, but even the slightest movement of his eyes made everything around him spin and swoop like he was on a roller coaster. "Ben, can you hear me? Look at me, Ben."

He concentrated as hard as he could, forcing his eyes to shift ever so slightly in her direction. Her blurry face hung over his.

"Good. Now, Ben, listen to me." Perillo was in full cop mode. "You're going to be okay. I've got you. You just stay with me and let me do the work. All you have to do is stay with me. If you understand me, just blink."

Ben struggled to close his eyes and then open them again. He was suddenly freezing and shivering, but soaked in sweat from head to toe.

"Great. Hero and I are going to get you out of here."

I don't want to leave, Ben tried to say, but it came out as a mumbled blur.

"Don't try to talk," Perillo said. "Save your energy." She pressed two fingers against his good wrist, checking his pulse.

"Dad . . ." Ben slurred.

"Shhhhh. You're in shock right now, Ben. What you're feeling—what your body is doing—is protecting you. Just let it happen. I'm here."

Ben felt Perillo lifting his head and neck slightly off the ground. She wrapped something around his shoulder and under his injured wrist, then tied it in a knot—creating a makeshift splint to stabilize his arm. Hero licked Ben's neck and face and snuffled into his ear, his warm breath brushing against Ben's cheek. Ben wanted to reach out his good arm to pet his dog, but he couldn't get it to move.

Hero looked at Perillo and began whimpering and yipping.

"Hero, sit," Perillo said. "Calm, buddy. Calm."

Hero quieted down but paced back and forth along the length of Ben's body, protecting him from any further harm.

Perillo spoke into her walkie-talkie again, telling dispatch to warn the closest hospital they were on their way. Next she radioed the helicopter pilot to meet them back where he had dropped them off—and to get ready to evacuate Ben.

Perillo leaned down over Ben and spoke to him gently. "Ben, listen. I'm going to pick you up now. And I'm going to carry you to the helicopter, and we're going to get you to the doctor, okay? Remember what I said? You're going to be fine."

Ben stared up at her, willing his mouth to move. He wanted to tell Perillo that he didn't care about himself—he didn't care about getting to the helicopter. He didn't care about his wrist or anything else except one thing: They were so close to finding his dad; they couldn't stop now.

Perillo raised Ben off the ground and heaved him over her left shoulder in a fireman's carry. She held on to his legs and pulled his head, chest, and one arm over her right shoulder.

A wave of nausea overcame him, and he shut his eyes.

Ben's head bounced up and down against her shoulder. He moved in and out of consciousness as she hauled him through the dense foliage. In the moments when he was awake, he was aware only of Perillo's labored breathing, the scorching pain in his arm, and Hero skittering along at Perillo's knees. Hero ran as close to Ben as possible without tripping Perillo.

Every few steps, Hero dashed ahead of Perillo for a moment, sniffing at the ground and redirecting them toward the helicopter. Then Hero would return to be close to Ben. Ben wished he could give Hero some kind of command—could be the alpha Hero needed—but at that moment, Hero was the one in charge, and Ben had never needed him more.

The pain in Ben's arm began to settle into a deep, steady throbbing. Waves of heat washed up and down from his wrist to his shoulder. A single thought came and went with the rhythm of the pain and Perillo's footsteps: *My dad. My dad. My dad.*

Slowly, that thought evolved in Ben's foggy brain.

A new thought arrived and receded, then returned. It was one word at first—*game*—then gradually expanded to become an idea: The game. The big game. The big game was coming up. And he was supposed to play in it.

He was supposed to pitch in the big game.

A fresh shot of adrenaline pumped through Ben's body, and for one split second before he passed out again, he became suddenly alert and acutely aware of one horrible fact: With this snakebite on his wrist, there was no way he could pitch in the playoff game in just a few days.

His team was relying on him.

And he was going to let them down.

10

BEN WOKE UNDER BRIGHT FLUORESCENT LIGHTS to the sound of dings and beeps and the whirring of machines. He felt something pressing against his leg.

He opened his eyes slowly, afraid that the tidal wave of nausea and vertigo would crash down on him again.

But there was nothing.

He was okay.

He opened his eyes fully and looked around. He was in a hospital room. His face was half covered by an oxygen mask, and his wrist—where the snake had bitten him—was wrapped in a thick bandage from the tips of his fingers to his elbow. He was hooked into a machine that blipped along with his heart rate and pulse.

Hero lay on the narrow hospital bed on Ben's good side, pressed snugly against his leg, his head resting on Ben's stomach. He had a "service dog" tag clipped to his collar. When Ben moved his head to look down at him, Hero half sat up and let out a happy yelp. He nosed Ben's armpit, licked his cheek next to the oxygen mask, and lay back down with his head on Ben's shoulder, his forehead pressed into Ben's neck.

The warmth of Hero's fur was like a familiar, soft blanket that warmed Ben up in the cold, bright room. The dizziness was gone, and the pain in his arm had subsided to a soft ache. But he was overcome with an exhaustion so deep he didn't know how it was possible to be this tired and awake at the same time.

His head felt extra heavy, but he raised it enough to look out the open door to his room. Officer Perillo stood just outside, talking animatedly on her cell phone. Her end of the conversation drifted across the room to him.

"That's great—when?" Perillo said into her phone. "Okay, they're on the move, then, and it sounds like they're moving fast. I'm heading out soon, but I just want to wait until . . ." She spun around to check on Ben. Her face lit up with a relieved smile when she saw that he was awake. "I have to go, Chief. I'll meet you at the rendezvous point."

She stuffed her phone into her pocket and crossed the room in a couple of quick steps.

"Ben! I'm so glad you're okay," Perillo said. "You gave me and Hero quite a scare out there."

Ben's mouth was dry, and his tongue felt like sandpaper. He used his good arm to lift the oxygen mask from his face. "Thank you," he managed to say. "You saved me."

"Well, I had a little help," Perillo replied, reaching down to scratch Hero's belly. Hero rolled onto his back and let out a happy sound. Perillo looked at Ben. "Ben, you were so brave tonight. Your dad is right about you."

"My—my dad. Is he . . . ?" Ben croaked.

Perillo sighed and pressed her lips tightly together. "We haven't found him—*yet*."

Ben squeezed his eyes shut in frustration. They had been so close—if he hadn't touched that rock, if he hadn't been bitten . . .

"It's not your fault, Ben," Perillo said, knowing

what he was thinking. "And besides, there's some good news. That was the chief on the phone just now. There was another ping from your dad's cell phone. They moved—they must have known we were close and headed farther west. But that means he's okay, Ben— he turned his phone on and off again."

"That's great," Ben mumbled.

"Let's put that back on, okay?" Perillo said, taking the mask from his hand and placing it back over his mouth and nose. "It's in the hands of the state police now. But they need us all on deck to back them up. I need to get back out there, Ben. You understand, right?"

Ben nodded.

"You're in the hospital outside of Hattiesburg, and you're going to be back on your feet in no time. The antivenom and painkillers they gave you are doing their job, and right now *your* job is to rest. It's the middle of the night, so I convinced your mom to stay home and get some sleep before driving up. She and Erin will be here bright and early. Until then, you've got Hero to keep you company."

Hero's ears danced back and forth on his head as he listened to Perillo speak, but his snout rested firmly on Ben's shoulder—keeping Ben safe in bed.

Ben reached up and gently eased Hero's head off his shoulder. He raised himself up on the elbow of his good arm. Hero snorted at him and readjusted himself on the tiny bed, hovering over Ben like a furry knight in shiny black armor.

"I'm coming with you," Ben said to Perillo. He swung his legs off the side of the bed and tried to sit up all the way.

Before Perillo could even try to talk him out of it, Ben let out a loud groan. He only made it a few inches toward a seated position when a flood of nausea barreled into him and the room spun like an amusement park ride. He flopped back onto the bed, clutching the sheets to try to stop the spinning.

Hero scooted closer to Ben and put a paw on his chest. There was no way he was letting Ben get up again.

"Looks like Hero and I are in agreement on this one," Perillo said, shaking her head gently. "Ben, that snake shot you up with a lot of venom, and now you're full of some seriously strong medication. You're going to start to feel better fast, but at the moment, the last thing you need to do is go running around the woods."

Ben had broken out in a cold sweat and couldn't

speak. He nodded slightly to let her know that he understood.

Perillo's phone dinged in her pocket.

"I'm sorry, but I have to go." She crossed the room but stopped and turned in the doorway. "Ben," Perillo said with a kind smile, "it's hard for me to imagine anyone but you and Hero saving the day. I know it's hard for you too. But listen, you need to rest. Promise me you'll do that—promise me you'll stay here and rest?"

Ben held her gaze. Finally, he nodded.

With a quick salute, Perillo slipped out the door and shut it softly behind her. As the room grew quiet, her words echoed in Ben's mind.

He had promised to stay put, but . . . Hero nuzzled at him. They looked at each other, and Ben felt like Hero was sharing his thoughts—as if the dog's deep, soulful eyes were trying to ask Ben something.

Ben thought he knew what it was. It was the same question that was running through his mind on repeat, until it became like a melody: *If not us, then who?*

If he and Hero didn't save his dad, who would?

Ben squeezed his eyes shut. Hero raised his head and licked Ben's face. His ears drooped low, and he looked about as sad and worried as Ben felt.

Ben didn't know if Hero was more upset that Ben was hurt or that they weren't out looking for his dad. Either way, he knew Hero would never leave his side.

The spinning and queasiness had subsided, but Ben's throat was tight with emotion. If he could have spoken, he would have told Hero that it was going to be okay. That Perillo and the other officers were going to find his dad as fast as possible. That they just had to put their trust in other people this time and hope for the best.

And in the meantime, the best thing they had was each other.

11

HERO DOZED OFF IN THE HOSPITAL bed. Ben could tell he was dreaming from the quick little snorts that escaped his nose and the way his legs twitched as if he were running in place. Hero's giant paws dug into Ben's ribs as they carried him around in his dreams—chasing a squirrel, maybe. Or a bad guy, more likely.

Ben couldn't sleep. It had been over an hour since Perillo left, and the hospital floor had gone stone silent as they reached the deadest part of night.

A nurse tiptoed into his room. She fiddled with the monitor attached to the various sensors clipped to him.

"Oh!" she said when she saw that Ben was awake.

"Sweetie, you need to sleep." Hero raised his head, sniffed the air around her, decided she wasn't a threat to Ben in any way, and dropped his head back onto Ben.

"I know," Ben said through the mask on his face.

"Are you thirsty?"

Ben nodded.

The nurse held up a small plastic water cup and lifted the straw to his lips. She pushed aside the mask, and he drank. The water was cool and delicious, and Ben felt it running through him, giving him strength.

The nurse checked her watch. "It'll be breakfast time soon enough. You're probably starving. I'll bring you some toast first thing, okay?"

"Thanks," Ben said. "That would be great."

The nurse tipped her head toward Hero. "And I'll see what I can find for him." She patted Ben's good arm. "Now try to sleep." She turned the lights off as she left the room.

But Ben was restless. He ran his fingers through Hero's fur and stared up at the ceiling, the events of the past twenty-four hours replaying in a speeding blur in his head.

First he was playing baseball, and the most important thing in the world—the only thing in the world—was the game. He was up at bat, he hit a home run . . . it was a glorious moment. All Ben cared about for a few minutes was winning the game and getting to the playoffs.

But how quickly things had changed again. As soon as they lost contact with his dad, baseball seemed so far away and unimportant. By morning, Ben's world had narrowed to a single fact: His dad was missing, and Ben wouldn't be able to think about or care about anything else until he was back, safe and sound.

They had been so close to finding him—just moments away. But then Ben had messed up and gotten himself hurt. And now here he was, stuck in the hospital, unable to do a thing.

If anything happened to his dad, it would be all Ben's fault. He had to figure out a way to help.

There was no way Ben was going to fall asleep.

Start with what you know, he heard his dad say. *That's what cops do. Don't worry about what you don't know—just work with what you've got. That's the first step toward figuring anything out.*

Ben's mind was spinning over the facts—and the absence of facts. He tried to break down what he knew: He knew his dad had been able to turn on his phone twice. That had to mean that the guys who had him didn't even realize he *had* a phone. Otherwise they would have taken it away.

Then there was what Ben didn't know: Why was his dad only able to turn it on and off for a couple of minutes at a time?

And there were the questions Ben didn't want to ask—let alone answer. What if the convicts found the phone before police officers got there—then what? They would take it away from his dad, sure, but what else would they do? Would they punish him for hiding it in the first place?

Ben pushed the thoughts away. *Don't focus on the fear,* his dad would say if he were here. *Focus only on the solution.*

One thing was clear: Staying here wasn't a solution—it was a waste of time.

Ben tried sitting up again, but this time he did it slowly. He made it onto his elbows without his head spinning, and he stayed there for a minute. Hero woke up with a start, his tags jingling on his collar. When he saw that Ben was trying to get up, he raised himself into a half crouch on Ben's bed.

Ben got himself up into a seated position. His

stomach churned a little, but he didn't feel like he was tumbling off the edge of the Earth this time.

Hero and Ben looked at each other. Ben put a hand on his dog's head. They stayed that way for a moment, Ben listening to the sounds out in the hallway, assessing who was around and what was happening. He heard the soft footsteps of the nurse walking by his door and fading as she headed down the hall. He heard a cart rolling down the long hallway. He heard a phone ringing at the nurses station a few yards away.

Then it was quiet.

Ben stood up slowly, carefully. He put his feet on the floor. It was cold, even through the hospital-issue socks with the rubber tread. He peeled off the medical equipment from his arm and swayed a little. Hero hopped off the bed and stood close enough to steady him.

Holding his bandaged arm in front of him, Ben took a few steps to the window, pulled aside the curtain, and looked out. Hero looked out with him, pressing his nose against the glass. Only the streetlights shined across the city. The houses and office buildings were dark and silent. There wasn't a soul in the parking lot a few stories below them. The moon was low in the sky.

Ben studied the purplish gray line in the distance

where the city skyline met the predawn sky. It would be daytime soon.

Perillo had said his mom and Erin would come first thing in the morning. If he knew his mom, she would be lying awake in her bed, waiting until it was light enough to come get him.

He and Hero needed to get out of there before she could stop them.

Ben found his clothes and backpack in the closet. Careful not to bump his injured arm, he got dressed as quickly as he could.

He gingerly eased the pack onto his shoulders. There was a sling hanging on the back of a chair. Ben pulled it over his neck and slid his arm into it.

They were ready to go. Now they just had to get past the nurses station.

Ben opened the door to his room and stuck his head out. He gave Hero the hand signal for *stay*. Ben looked up and down the corridor. About ten yards to his right, a doctor leaned against the nurses' desk, writing notes in a chart. His back was turned ever so slightly to Ben. There were no nurses in sight.

Ben slipped out the door and gestured for Hero to come. They headed left down the hall, toward the glowing red exit sign. Ben half expected to hear some-one calling his name. But they made it to the stairwell door without being stopped.

Ben was still not totally steady on his feet. He stopped on each landing to rest, while Hero sniffed around the stairwell. After what felt like an eternity, they emerged in the back of a large lobby, where one lone security guard sat at a desk at the front of the room. From where Ben was standing, it seemed pretty certain that the guy was sound asleep.

Ben and Hero stepped through a revolving door and into the parking lot. Leaning against the back wall of the building, Ben pulled up a navigation app on his phone and oriented himself.

Perillo had said that his dad's phone pinged just west of where they had found the campfire. According to the map, the hospital was just a little bit farther west of that. If Hero and Ben headed east, they would reach the right spot and Hero could find Ben's dad.

They made their way across the parking lot just as the sky lightened to a pink-gray. When they got to the edge of the lot, Ben stopped, pulled something from his backpack, and held it under Hero's nose.

Then he gave his dog the most important command he'd ever given: "Hero, find Dad."

Hero sniffed the sweatshirt, turned, and sniffed at the ground and the air. He began walking.

Behind him, Ben stepped out onto the road.

They turned east and were on their way again.

12

BEN FOUGHT THE FATIGUE THAT COURSED through his body.

After the initial burst of adrenaline as he and Hero busted out of the hospital, the effects of the snake venom—and all the medicine he'd been given to counteract it—had returned. Each foot felt like it weighed a hundred pounds, and every step took immense effort. He trudged down the road. Hero slowed his pace so Ben could keep up. He stopped every few yards, looked back at Ben, and waited.

The sun had come up quickly. It was a bright, cool morning, and they walked on a sleepy residential street. The sun was soothing and warm on Ben's face after the long night in the dark woods and a chilly hospital room.

It was Sunday, and only a few early risers were out on their porches, grabbing the morning paper or sipping coffee in their bathrobes. They'd wave at Ben, and he'd give a weak half wave with his good hand. As Ben and Hero walked, the houses grew sparser, with more land between them.

They were getting closer to the edge of the woods.

They hadn't traveled more than a mile when Ben had to stop.

"Wait, Hero," he said. Ben dropped onto the curb to rest.

Hero doubled back, his nails clacking on the asphalt. He stopped in front of Ben, his tail up and his brow furrowed. Hero barked once.

"I know, buddy," Ben said. "I want to get there too. But I just need a second."

Hero whined and pranced a little with his front paws. He ran a few feet away, in the direction they had been heading, then stopped and looked back.

Ben put his head down on his knees to steady himself, gathering his strength. A wave of nausea passed, and he felt energy returning to his limbs. He needed to get himself up off the curb and back on his feet. Hero was his dad's best shot, and right now, Ben was keeping Hero from helping.

"Your dog looks like he's in a hurry," came a voice from nearby.

Ben's head shot up.

A boy straddled a bike in the road and stared at them. He was about Ben's age, with shaggy brown hair and glasses. He was wearing jeans and an Atlanta Braves sweatshirt.

"Um, yeah," Ben said, his voice hoarse.

"Why?"

Ben wasn't sure how to answer that.

Even if he wanted to tell a stranger about his dad, the escaped convicts, the snakebite, and Hero's search-and-rescue skills, there was no way this kid would believe him.

Ben didn't need to worry about what to say, though. The boy wasn't waiting for an answer.

"You in some kind of trouble?" the kid asked.

"No—not really," Ben said. He realized as he said it how unconvincing he sounded.

"You kind of look like you're in trouble."

Hero wandered back to Ben and sat down in front of him—placing himself between Ben and the stranger. He eyed the boy suspiciously.

Ben stood up, trying hard not to look too unsteady. He could see the boy on the bike taking mental notes of his bandaged arm, his heavy backpack.

Ben felt like he was under a microscope.

"Can I help you?" Ben asked.

The boy shrugged. "Seems like you're the one who needs help."

"I'm fine," Ben said. "We were just taking a break. But we're gonna get going now. Come on, Hero." Ben took a few slow steps.

"Okay. Bye, then." The boy put his feet on the pedals and cycled slowly in a wide circle, heading off in the opposite direction.

Ben took a few more steps. His arm began to throb, and he felt like he was going to collapse. He stopped, put his good hand on his knee, and took a few deep breaths.

A thought occurred to him. He stood up and called after the kid.

"Hey—"

The boy jammed on his brakes and looked over his shoulder at Ben.

"Yeah?"

"You know what? You were right. We do need help."

The boy didn't say anything.

"We have to get into the forest kind of quickly," Ben went on. "It's super important. And I'm not feeling so hot. I . . . uh . . . I got bit by a snake last night."

The boy still said nothing. He just stared at Ben, waiting.

"And, well, um . . ." Ben said, "I'm having a hard time walking."

Finally, the boy spoke. "Yeah, I can see that."

Ben wasn't sure what to make of this kid. Was he being serious—or was he totally messing with him?

"So," Ben went on, "it sure would be a lot easier if I had a bike. What do you say I borrow yours, and I'll bring it back to you later today? I can pay you." He dug in his pocket and pulled out his wallet. A scrap of orange fabric fell out with it and floated to the ground. As quickly as he could, Ben picked it up and shoved it back in his pocket. He checked his wallet for cash. He had a ten and a five. "I can give you fifteen dollars now. But as soon as we find my dad"—Ben regretted including that detail the second it came out of his mouth—"I can give you more."

The boy kept staring at Ben. His eyes were big and unblinking.

Ben waited.

Had the kid even heard the offer? Did Ben need to repeat himself?

"No."

Ben opened his mouth to respond, then realized he had no idea what to say and closed it again.

"But I can get you a bike." The boy pushed his glasses up the bridge of his nose and stared at Ben some more.

Ben was flooded with relief. "Great!" He turned and walked toward the kid. "Let's go. Hero and I are in a serious hurry."

"It's just over there," the boy said, pointing back toward the last house on the block. "We'll grab it real quick. Then we'll get going."

Ben stopped in his tracks.

"We?"

Hero looked from Ben to the kid and back again.

"I'm coming with you." The boy spoke as if it were a fact.

Ben shook his head. "I'm sorry—I didn't mean that I needed *your* help. I just meant that I need a bike so I could move faster."

The boy didn't say anything.

"Thanks anyway," Ben went on, foundering for words, "Hero and I would rather go on our own. So . . . where's that bike?"

"Well, I can't give you the bike"—the boy shrugged—"unless I can come with you."

Ben thought he would lose his mind with frustration. The clock was ticking, and he was wasting precious time talking to a kid he didn't even know. He took a few deep breaths so he wouldn't say anything he would regret.

"We don't need you to come with us," Ben said. "But I'll still pay you for the bike."

"I don't need your money," the boy said. "But where you're going, you're going to need me."

"You know what? Forget it." Ben didn't have time to play games. He waved a dismissive hand in the kid's direction, turned, and headed slowly back toward the forest, Hero close by his side.

"Have a nice walk."

Ben could feel the boy's eyes on his back. He'd only

gone a few feet, but his arm was already pulsing with a dull pain and his legs felt like jelly.

"These are my woods," the kid called after him. "I can get you there faster than you can get there on your own."

Ben stopped. He sighed. He shook his head. But he couldn't argue with the chance to get to his dad faster. He turned slowly and looked at the boy.

"Fine. But can we please get going?"

A huge grin spread across the kid's face. "Follow me!"

The boy slowly pedaled his bike while Ben and Hero walked beside him. "I'm Tucker. What's your name?"

"Ben."

"That's Hero?"

"Yeah. That's Hero," Ben said.

They turned into the driveway, and Tucker pulled around the back of the house. Hero sniffed at the grass and gravel. At the far edge of the yard, a jungle gym and an aboveground pool sat empty.

Ben looked around. There was only one bike leaning against the back of the house: a pink-and-white Schwinn with a long narrow seat, rainbow streamers dangling from the handles, and a white wicker basket with a pink kitten face—complete with whiskers—hanging off the front.

"There's your bike," Tucker said.

Ben sighed. "Let me guess. It's your little sister's?"

"Yup."

"Fine, let's go." Ben could not have cared less about the bike. He would have ridden a purple unicorn with feathers if it meant they could get going. He hopped on the bike, which was at least five inches too short for him. Steering with his one good arm, he started to pedal down the driveway. His knees nearly hit him in the face as he rode the tiny bike.

"Hang on," Tucker said. "I need to get my supplies."

Ben screeched to a halt. "Your supplies—are you kidding me?!" Ben couldn't hide his frustration. "This isn't a camping trip! I need to get going. My dad is in trouble, and he needs me and Hero *right now*!"

"Okay, okay, sorry." Tucker threw his hands up in apology. "I'll hurry." He ran into the house through the back door and returned a couple of minutes later carrying an open backpack in one hand.

In the other, he held a fistful of items, including a water bottle and a plastic bag full of something shriveled and brown. "You hungry?" He held out the plastic bag in Ben's direction. "I've got some jerky." Hero sniffed at it and turned away.

A sharp, pungent smell drifted toward Ben. He gritted his teeth and shook his head. "I'm good, thanks."

Tucker shoved all the items into his pack, zipped it shut, tossed it onto his shoulders, and hopped on his bike in one smooth motion.

"You ready?" Ben asked with an impatient exhale.

"Sure am." Tucker grinned.

With an eye roll, Ben rode down the driveway and turned onto the quiet, empty street. Tucker rode next to him.

Hero ran out ahead of them both. He picked up speed effortlessly, his muscular legs working in rhythm as he ran at full tilt, leading the way back into the woods.

13

BEN ANGLED HIS KNEES OUT TO the side and scooted as far back as he could on the banana seat. As much as he would have liked to have Noah's and Jack's help finding his dad, he was glad they weren't there to point out how dorky he looked at that moment.

As awkward as it was, the bike was still better—and quicker—than walking. And if it would get him to his dad even a minute faster, then he didn't care if he looked like a rodeo clown.

They rode down the middle of a deserted street with no houses. Ben was starting to feel a little less wiped out, and his arm wasn't throbbing quite so much. Mostly he was relieved to be moving again.

He pedaled silently a few feet ahead of Tucker, who was riding along at a steady but decidedly not fast pace behind him. Hero dashed out ahead of them, his nose low to the ground and his tail up. Every few minutes, Hero stopped and waited for them to catch up.

Ben didn't know if dogs could actually feel impatient, but if they did, then Hero was as impatient as could be. If Hero could roll his eyes, Ben was pretty sure that's what he would have been doing.

"Is he . . . tracking?" Tucker called out ahead to Ben.

"Yeah," Ben replied. "He's a search-and-rescue dog. That's what he does."

Tucker pedaled quickly so he could ride side by side with Ben.

So he can *ride faster,* Ben thought.

"He any good at it?" Tucker asked. "He looks like he's pretty good at it."

"He's the best. He was on the police force with my dad."

"Your dad's a cop?"

"Yeah."

"That how he ended up missing?"

"I never said he was missing."

"No. But you said you were going to find him. And you said you were in a hurry. And you seem pretty stressed out. So I'm just doing the math, that's all. And to me, it all adds up to your dad being missing."

Ben had to give it to Tucker. He was smart—and observant. "Yeah, he's missing," Ben admitted. "Since the night before last. He was out looking for these two escaped convicts—"

"I saw them on the news," Tucker said, a look of understanding spreading across his face as he pieced Ben's whole story together. "Your dad is the guy they took?"

"Yeah." Ben swallowed the knot in his throat.

"Wow. That sucks."

"It sucks a lot."

They rode in silence for a while. When they finally reached the edge of the woods, Hero charged right into the trees. Ben and Tucker followed, riding along a narrow dirt path. Ben tried to pick up the pace, but Tucker lagged behind.

Ben wasn't going to wait around for him. He pedaled as fast as he could, even though the bumping and jostling made his arm ache. If Tucker didn't want to keep up, that was his problem.

Ben kept his eyes on Hero and steered one-handed.

He heard the sound of Tucker's tires on the dirt right behind him. Suddenly Tucker pulled up next to Ben.

"Hero—is he tracking your dad right now?"

"Well, he's trying to find his scent," Ben replied. "He's catching tens of thousands of different smells right now—way more than we ever could."

Tucker looked impressed. "That's pretty cool." He started to drop back behind Ben again.

"Listen, Tucker," Ben said over his shoulder. "I appreciate your help and all, but Hero and I really need to hurry. So I'm just gonna go on ahead, okay?"

"No problem," Tucker said from behind him.

Hero had become a faraway speck in the woods. Ben double-timed it, trying not to lose sight of him. "Hero," he called out, his voice strong and clear, like Perillo had coached him. "Stay close, buddy." Hero slowed his pace a drop so Ben could keep up.

"I could ride with you," Tucker called out from behind him. "But that wouldn't help us get there any faster."

Ben squeezed his eyes shut for a moment, trying to keep his cool—Tucker wasn't even making sense. He opened them again. "What do you mean?" he called out over his shoulder.

"I mean, if we go too fast, then I can't pay attention."

"Pay attention to what?"

"Same kind of stuff Hero pays attention to, only not with my nose. Like, for example, footprints. Tree branches that were snapped or messed with. Cigarette butts. Gum wrappers."

Ben's head shot up at "gum wrappers." "Did you already see something?"

"Sure I did."

Ben skidded to a stop and waited for Tucker to ride up next to him. "What did you see?" Ben asked excitedly.

"Some old soda cans. A spot where someone definitely lay down for a while. Oh, and a gum wrapper."

Ben's heart pounded in his chest. "Was it Big Red?"

"It was," Tucker said. "Does that mean something?"

"It means," Ben said, pedaling again, "that we're going the right way."

They rode side by side, the wind whistling in Ben's ears as they went.

"Keep your voice down," Ben said softly. "We could be getting close to them."

Tucker nodded. His face was serious as he scanned

the trees around them, looking for signs of the two convicts—and Ben's dad.

"How do you know what to look for?" Ben whispered.

Tucker shrugged. "I've been coming here every day my entire life. I just . . . notice stuff." He was quiet for a moment, deep in thought. "Could your dad's scent have been on someone who was with your dad?"

Ben thought for a moment, reviewing everything he'd learned about tracking since Hero had come to live with him. "I guess so."

"Well," Tucker said. "Then that makes more sense."

"What makes more sense?"

"I only see one set of boot prints. And I doubt they're your dad's, because if he'd come this far toward the edge of the woods, he would have seen the road we just came from and gone for help. So I think Hero was picking up his scent on someone else."

As Tucker said it, Hero came to a sudden stop up ahead, turned around, and galloped through the trees back toward them. Ben and Tucker slammed on their brakes. Hero crossed the path to Ben, sat down, and waited for a command.

Ben knew that could mean only one thing.

Hero didn't have his dad's scent.

Panic rose in Ben's chest. He wanted to scream in frustration, but he forced himself to take a few deep breaths instead. He exhaled slowly. *Breathe,* he could hear his dad telling him. *You can be afraid later.*

Tucker watched as Ben frantically pulled his dad's sweatshirt from his backpack and held it under Hero's nose again.

"Hero lost his scent?" Tucker asked. Ben nodded, too upset to speak. "No big deal," Tucker said.

Ben clenched and unclenched his fists. The movement sent a sharp jolt of pain through his wounded arm. He breathed. He counted to ten. He asked himself what his dad would do in this situation.

Nothing worked. Ben could no longer hold back the wave of emotions swelling in him, and he turned on Tucker.

"No big deal?! No big deal?" Ben spat. "What are you saying, Tucker? This is a huge deal! Do you not get that my dad is in danger?"

"Whoa—Ben, sorry," Tucker held out his hands in an apologetic gesture. "I didn't mean to upset you. I just meant that it's no big deal because there's another way to find your dad."

Ben stared at Tucker, blood still pounding in his ears. He opened and closed his mouth a couple of times until he found the right words. "I'm sorry," Ben said simply. His cheeks were hot with embarrassment and anger. "I'm just really stressed out right now. What do you mean there's another way?"

Tucker didn't seem fazed by Ben's outburst. "Hero gets the person's scent off an item, right?" he asked.

Ben nodded.

"So couldn't he track the prisoners instead of your dad? I mean, if they have your dad, then following them should lead you right to him."

"I mean—yes, but—I don't get it." Ben wasn't following Tucker's point. That was logical—*if* they had a scent item that either of the prisoners had touched.

"Orange fabric," Tucker said matter-of-factly.

"What?" Ben had no idea what he was talking about.

"The little piece of orange fabric that's in your pocket. I saw you drop it earlier. That's from one of the prisoners, right?"

Ben jammed his hand into his pocket and pulled

out the shred of cloth. It curled up in his palm. He looked up at Tucker in amazement. "You're right," he said.

Ben hopped off the tiny bike and crouched down next to Hero. Ben held the cloth under Hero's nose. Hero sniffed at it, cleared his nose with a sharp snort, then sniffed some more. He ran his nose over it again and again. Finally he looked up at Ben.

Hero was ready.

"Good boy," Ben said. He gave Hero a treat.

"He sniffs that, and then he's good to go?" Tucker asked.

"That's right."

Tucker nodded appreciatively. "Now what?"

"Now this." Ben looked at Hero and scratched him under the collar. "Hero, FIND IT!"

Hero shot out into the woods. Ben and Tucker pedaled fast to keep up.

The woods got denser; the trees grew closer together, and their foliage formed a tight canopy far above the boys' heads. The bright daylight dimmed, making it harder for Ben and Tucker to navigate the bumpy trail on their bikes.

They trailed Hero as closely as they could. Hero moved with his usual deftness and grace, weaving around trees and leaping over rocks at top speed without a hint of effort. But Ben could tell that Hero was still upset, still as desperate to find Ben's dad as Ben was. Hero had the same raw energy that he'd had the night before.

This time, though, Ben knew what to do. And he knew that Hero needed him to take the lead and guide him.

When Hero got too far ahead of them, his movements quick and frenzied, his head low to the ground, Ben shouted, "Hero, stay close!" in a strong and firm voice that came from his gut.

Each time, Hero slowed his pace so the boys could catch up. Ben and Tucker bounced over rocks, ducked under low branches, and swerved around thick tree stumps. Tucker was right beside Ben now, not hanging back.

Ben thought about this person he'd just met. He could safely say Tucker was unlike anyone he'd ever known before. The kid was some kind of cross between a mind reader and a woodsman—a kind of nature superhero. Ben turned his head slightly and watched Tucker pedaling hard on his bike, his glasses covered with specks of dirt and his hair flapping in the wind.

Despite the seriousness of their mission, Ben had to laugh as a thought occurred to him: Tucker was the boy equivalent of Hero.

Just then, Hero slowed to a near stop. His snout hovered a few inches above the underbrush, and he crept forward carefully, one paw at a time. His body tensed, and his ears moved back on his head.

Ben knew that Hero had stumbled upon a new scent—something that hadn't been there even seconds before.

For Ben, the woods smelled like a lovely mix of piney bark, rich soil, and wet leaves. For Hero, that didn't even begin to scratch the surface.

To Hero's precise, highly sophisticated nose, the woods were a complex stew of thousands and thousands of scents that wove in and around one another, mixing together and separating again. As he ran and listened and looked, Hero also absorbed, differentiated, and sorted every one of those scents into different categories—all while he kept his senses finely tuned for the one they were looking for.

It was a herculean task by any measure, but for Hero, it was as natural as breathing.

Ben and Tucker slowed down and watched Hero work. Soon Hero corrected his path and led them on a new trajectory—at top speed. Ben and Tucker picked up the pace.

They worked their way deeper and deeper into the shadowy woods. As the sunlight grew dimmer and the air took on a damp chill, Ben couldn't shake a creeping sensation.

He had the definite feeling that someone, somewhere, was watching them.

They weren't alone.

14

THE UNDERGROWTH HAD BECOME A THICK carpet of tree roots and ropy vines crisscrossing the ground. The path had disappeared.

It was too hard to ride their bikes any longer. Ben and Tucker hopped off and stashed them behind a tall pile of brush, where they couldn't be easily seen by anyone walking by. The boys made a solemn promise to return for the bikes as soon as they could.

"Trust me," Tucker said with a sigh, "you would not want to be there when my sister found out I lost her bike."

They moved forward on foot. Ben's body was stiff and sore, but he was definitely stronger—and less dizzy—than he had been earlier. His arm still hurt, but he was slowly starting to feel like himself again.

As they walked, Tucker wordlessly pointed to things Ben wouldn't have noticed on his own: A trail of crushed leaves, where a large animal—a bear or a buck—had walked not long before they came through. A snake curled around a tree branch, totally still and nearly invisible. Ben shuddered at the very sight of it.

They passed a few crumbling, camouflaged hunting cabins tucked among the trees. Each time they spotted one, Tucker signaled to Ben to stop and wait while he checked it out. Tucker would silently slip around the side of the shack and peer through a window to look in.

They were all empty.

The boys walked quietly for a long while, their feet falling into a steady rhythm. Hero forged ahead with total focus. He never seemed to get tired or winded.

Ben felt the cool air through his jacket. He kept an eye on the sky as they trekked farther and farther east. The day had started to turn flat and gray, and the sun fought to make its way out from behind a blanket of clouds.

Ben's mind swam with thoughts of his dad. Had

Perillo and the others found anything yet? Were they even getting closer? Was his dad safe?

He checked his phone. There was no service, which meant no news—and no word from his mom. Had she gotten to the hospital yet and realized that Ben was missing? It was something he couldn't worry about right now. He had to focus.

But Ben was tired and sore, and growing hungrier by the minute. A terrible feeling sprouted in his gut—a feeling he didn't recognize at first. It was a feeling he didn't want to admit to having: hopelessness.

Ben pushed the thought away with every bit of strength he had left. Losing hope for this mission meant losing hope for his dad—and that was something he would never, ever do, no matter how frustrated or exhausted he felt.

He thought back to something his dad had often told him: The best way to make a case go badly was to expect it to go well. *Cops can never think things will go the way we want them to,* his dad had said many times. *We have to assume that things will be as hard as they can possibly be. Any case can fall apart at any moment. If we don't remember that, we get careless.*

"Tell me about your dad." Tucker interrupted Ben's thoughts.

"What do you want to know?" Ben asked.

"I don't know—he sounds kind of cool," Tucker said.

"He's . . ." Ben trailed off, searching for the right words. "He's great. He's, you know, tough on me, but not in a crazy way. He pushes me."

"What's it like having a cop for a dad—is it hard?"

Ben wasn't sure how to answer that at first, because he'd never known anything different. He thought for a moment. "No. I mean, he's pretty protective," Ben said. "And I can't lie—like, ever—because he can totally tell. And it can be scary—sometimes his job is dangerous." He chuckled as he said it. "I guess that's an understatement considering where we are right now."

Tucker laughed. "I guess."

Ben waited for the sadness to kick in again, like it had last night when Perillo was talking about his dad. But it didn't happen this time. Instead it felt good to talk about him—it helped somehow.

"Has he always had a police dog?" Tucker asked.

"For as long as I can remember, anyway. He's called

a K-9 officer. Hero was his partner, but then Hero retired, so now he's my dog."

"That's cool," Tucker said. He was quiet for a moment. "My dad's not around. My stepdad is okay, I guess."

Ben felt like a jerk for going on about how great his own father was. "Sorry—I didn't mean . . ." he trailed off. "That must be tough."

"Nah," Tucker said. "I'm used to it. My mom is really happy since she met him. So that's good. But he's not my dad, you know?"

"Where is your dad?"

"He lives in Atlanta." Tucker changed the subject. "You hungry?"

Ben's stomach gurgled at the mere mention of food. He couldn't remember ever being this hungry before. He'd eaten his last granola bar for breakfast.

"I'm starving," he admitted. "But I'm out of food."

"Lucky for you"—Tucker grinned—"I have plenty of jerky. Want to rest for a sec?"

Ben's legs were tired. A rest sounded great, but he also just wanted to keep moving.

"I can eat and walk," Ben said.

"Suit yourself." Tucker pulled his backpack around

to his chest and began digging through it while they walked. He pulled out the plastic bag full of dried meat and held it out to Ben.

It looked stringy and dark. Under normal circumstances, it wasn't something Ben would be enthusiastic about eating, but he didn't want to be rude—and he had no idea when or where his next meal would be.

Tucker opened the bag, and the sharp smell rose from it and drifted toward Ben. Even Hero raised his head as the odor reached him in the distance.

Ben stuck a hand into the bag and took a small piece. Tucker watched him carefully as he raised it to his mouth and took a bite.

The jerky was tough and dry, and when he bit into it, a burst of musky meatiness filled his mouth. It was somehow bland and overpowering at the same time.

It was the most disgusting thing he had ever tasted in his entire life.

Ben was overcome with a powerful urge to eject the food from his mouth, but he forced himself to keep chewing. All the while, Tucker watched him, an expectant look on his face.

"Well, what do you think?" Tucker asked.

Ben thought he was going to barf.

When he couldn't take it for another second, Ben gagged and spat the chewed-up jerky into the dirt by his feet.

"I'm sorry, dude," Ben said, wiping his tongue on his sleeve. "I don't mean to be rude, but I can't eat this." He took a swig of water, swished it around in his mouth, and spat that out too. "That is . . . That is . . ." Ben fumbled for the right words.

"That's my grandma's recipe," Tucker said, looking crushed.

Ben felt terrible. "Oh, man—I didn't mean to . . . I'm so sorry . . . I—"

Tucker burst out laughing. "Oh, man, you should see your face! It's priceless!"

Ben was confused for a second, but soon Tucker was doubled over laughing, and Ben couldn't help laughing along with him.

"Wait," Ben said, "are you telling me you know how nasty that stuff is?"

"Oh yeah. It's disgusting, right?" Tucker could hardly breathe he was laughing so hard. Tears streamed down his cheeks.

"What is it?"

"It's venison jerky," Tucker managed to say between

bursts of laughter. "My grandma makes it by the pound."

Hero stopped running and turned back to see what the commotion was. He cocked his head to the side and cast a suspicious eye on Tucker.

Ben was laughing almost as hard as Tucker now. "How do you eat it if it's so bad?"

"I don't know," Tucker said, wiping his cheeks and catching his breath. "I guess I'm just used to it. They've been making me eat it since I was a little kid. Everyone hates it, but we all eat it. We have to."

Ben shook his head. "That's insane!"

"Totally," Tucker said. "But no one wants to hurt Granny's feelings. And it has tons of protein so it's great for camping."

Hero barked at Ben.

"It's okay, pal," Ben said. "But if you're looking for lunch, you do not want to eat that."

"Sorry, Hero," Tucker said, "but Ben's right." He stopped walking. "Tell you what, though—how would you like some nice fresh fish?"

"Are you carrying a bass around in your backpack?" Ben asked. "Because I don't see any water around here."

"Just wait." Tucker grinned. "Follow me."

He led them off the trail and over a small rise. A little ways beyond it, a stream flowed and burbled. Tucker sat down on a large, flat rock that formed a perfect bench, his feet dangling over the water. "Fish coming right up."

"How are you going to catch them?" Ben asked, dropping down next to him. His whole body thanked him for taking a break. Hero trotted down to the water's edge and lapped up some of the cool water. "Because I'm pretty sure you don't have a fishing rod in there either."

"Aha." Tucker reached back into his pack and pulled out a short stick that ended in a Y shape, with a thin strip of rubber connecting the ends. "That's what this is for."

It was a handmade slingshot. Ben studied it as Tucker turned it over, held it in one hand, and tugged on the piece of rubber with the other. He palmed a small, round rock about the size of a walnut.

"No way," Ben said. "You can't actually catch a fish with that, can you?"

"Sure can," Tucker said. "Watch."

He lay on his stomach on the flat rock, perched up on his elbows, and pulled the rubber band taut. He slipped the rock into the band, squinted, and eyed the fish swimming back and forth underwater. Ben held his breath and watched.

Tucker stayed frozen in one position for so long that Ben thought maybe he was messing with him again. Then, suddenly, before Ben even knew that Tucker had let go of the rubber band, there was a pop, and a whizzing sound, and a *plink* as the rock sliced into the water at top speed.

Bubbles rose to the surface, but otherwise, there was no indication that anything had happened. Ben was about to tease Tucker when the other boy hopped off the rock and jumped down to the water's edge. He took a couple of steps into the stream, bent down, stuck his hand in, and stood up gripping a fat, squirming catfish.

"Here you go," Tucker said. "Lunch."

Ben's jaw fell open. "Wow. That was amazing."

"Guess you probably want this cooked for you, city boy," Tucker joked. "Let me just light a fire."

"Ha." Ben rolled his eyes. "Thanks, but I can handle that part."

While Tucker caught another catfish, Ben took off his pack and gathered dried wood, holding it carefully in the crook of his bandaged arm. He formed a small pyramid on the flat rock and stuffed kindling around the bottom. Holding a matchbox in his injured hand, he struck a match with the other.

Ben's mouth watered as the fish cooked over the open fire, but he was painfully aware of how much time was passing. He felt jittery with hunger and a desire to keep moving. They had to eat—but they also had to hurry.

Tucker, on the other hand, seemed totally unconcerned with how slowly the food was cooking. He leaned back on his pack, watching the fish turning on the end of the stick in his hand.

"It looks done," Ben said, peering over.

"Almost. Just needs another minute."

Hero was just as anxious as Ben was. The dog paced nearby, his tail down and his ears hanging low around his head.

"It's okay, buddy," Ben said. "We're gonna get going soon."

"Here you go," Tucker said, handing Ben the stick at last. Ben placed the crispy, steaming fish down on the rock in front of him to let it cool. Hero popped over and sniffed at what was about to be their shared lunch.

Within minutes, Ben was full, and Hero was licking his chops in satisfaction. Tucker was taking his time finishing his meal, wiping his mouth on his sleeve between bites.

Ben put his head down on his backpack and looked up at the small puzzle pieces of sky visible beyond the treetops. Hero lay down next to him.

Impatience coursed through Ben. *I should stand up,* he thought. *I should get my pack on and show Tucker I'm ready.*

Hero was warm next to Ben. His fur was soft. Ben's belly was full. The leaves on the trees danced in the breeze and made a soft rustling sound.

I'm going to get up right now, Ben thought as his heavy eyelids closed. *After I rest my eyes for a second.*

15

BEN'S BACK HURT; HE WAS LYING on something cold and hard. His arm was throbbing and tightly wrapped. He had no idea where he was—only that he was staring up into darkness and trees. Hero dozed next to him. Water burbled nearby.

Then it all came crashing back: His dad. The snakebite. The hospital. And now he and Hero were out in the woods with Tucker, heading east to find his dad.

But why was it dark out? Hadn't it just been lunchtime?

Ben sat up, rubbed his face with his hands, and looked around. Across from him, Tucker leaned against his backpack, gazing into the fire. Ben groggily remembered the slingshot and the fish. He recalled the fatigue that had overcome him after he ate . . .

He had fallen asleep.

"How long have I been sleeping?" Ben panicked. "We have to go! It's dark—what time is it? My dad—"

"It's okay, Ben," Tucker said. "You were pretty wiped out. I didn't want to wake you up."

Tucker really didn't seem to understand the urgency of the situation.

"If your dad was missing," Ben snapped, unable to control his frustration, "I think you'd have woken me up!"

"Whoa. That's not cool." Tucker sounded hurt.

Ben remembered what Tucker had told him about his dad—how he barely ever saw him.

"I'm sorry," Ben said, dropping his head into his hands. "That was lame. I didn't mean— I'm just . . . I'm sorry."

"Don't worry about it." Tucker stood up and brushed off his jeans. He started kicking ashes onto the fire to put it out. "Let's get going."

"Tucker, seriously. I'm sorry."

Tucker stopped and looked up at Ben. "You're lucky to have a dad like yours."

Ben was silent as they set off again, Hero in the lead.

They walked along the edge of the stream. Hero sniffed at the slippery rocks and waded into the water, splashing along and constantly searching for the scent he'd found on the scrap of orange fabric.

"He can even follow a scent in water?" Tucker asked, watching Hero work.

"He can," Ben said.

"Can all dogs do that?"

"Track over water? Special ones, like Hero."

Tucker looked impressed. "Bet that comes in handy."

Ben was relieved that Tucker didn't seem angry at him for his outburst. "It does. Last year, Hero and I were stuck out in the forest during the hurricane with my friends—"

"During the actual hurricane?" Tucker interrupted.

"Yeah." Ben felt ridiculous saying it out loud. It sounded crazy now, but at the time, he hadn't felt like he had a choice . . . It was the same way he had felt when he left the hospital earlier that morning to find his dad. "My friend Jack got stuck in the woods with his dog, Scout." Hero's ears popped up at the sound of Scout's name. "And we couldn't just leave them out there alone."

"It must have been pretty wild out there during the storm."

Ben shrugged. "I guess. But I was just way more worried about finding Jack and Scout. Plus, I had Hero to keep me safe."

"Hero," Tucker called out to the dog, "you're pretty cool." Hero wagged his tail and kept walking. "So what happened to Scout?" he asked Ben.

"Actually," Ben said, "Scout is my dad's new partner. He's out there with my dad right now. Hero helped train him. He's going to become either a police dog or a military dog."

"What's, like, the craziest rescue Hero ever made?" Tucker asked.

"Hard to say." Ben thought for a moment. "I mean, during the hurricane, he found a Boy Scout troop trapped in a cave. And then this one Boy Scout and I got stuck in a really strong current after the flooding . . ."

Ben trailed off, worried he was going on too much.

"So what happened?" Tucker urged him on.

"Well . . ." Ben ran through the dozens of stories he could tell about Hero's amazing career—including the one about Hero finding Ben as a little kid, lost and alone in the woods at night. Every time he finished one rescue story, Tucker begged him for another.

When Ben had run through the best rescue stories, Tucker asked him for Hero's craziest arrests and take-downs. Ben told him the one about the bank robber. Then the ones about the car thief and the guy who stole things from people's front porches. And the one about the dogfighting ring—which Ben and Hero had busted up together.

There were just so many to choose from, but Tucker didn't seem to get bored.

They trekked through the dark for a couple more miles. The moon was high overhead. Dim moonlight shone down through the leaves, creating a patchwork of light and shadow.

Tucker slowed his pace and gestured to Ben to slow down too. Tucker raised a finger to his lips to shush him.

At the same moment, Hero froze midstep. He lifted his head, his ears up, and scanned the area around them carefully. His tail extended straight out behind him. Ben watched Hero for any indication of what he might have smelled or heard.

Tucker tapped Ben on the arm and pointed at a large, flat rock nearby. Ben squinted in the dim light and saw what looked like a short tower on top of it. He stepped closer and saw that it was a pile of three small rocks that had been carefully—and intentionally—stacked one on top of the other.

Ben looked at Tucker in silent confusion.

"It's a signal," Tucker whispered. "Hikers and hunters do it to let other people know there's trouble."

Ben went cold. Had his dad placed those there while the escaped prisoners weren't watching?

If so, what kind of a warning was he sending? Were the convicts the trouble, or was it something else entirely?

They forged ahead for another half mile, Ben and Tucker moving as silently as possible, trying not to step on any branches. Hero moved as quickly and stealthily as ever. Ben felt the ground sloping upward as he walked, until they stood at the top of a small hill.

"There," Tucker whispered, pointing to a spot just below them. Ben followed his finger but couldn't see anything in the thick woods at first. He saw only leaves and trees, then more leaves and trees.

Ben scanned the tree line again, and this time he

spotted it, as if it were suddenly emerging from the natural world around it: a dilapidated hunting shack nestled among the trees, its rough plank walls blending in perfectly with the forest around it.

"That's Old Man Scoggins's shack," Tucker said quietly. "He doesn't come out here anymore. No one in his family does. It should be empty." Tucker's voice was low and calm, but Ben saw that he was taking in the whole scene—the shack, the tall trees surrounding it on three sides, the darkness between the tree trunks. Ben recognized something in Tucker's expression. It was an alertness, a sharp-eyed observation that he'd often seen in his dad and in Hero.

Tucker reached for the slingshot in his back pocket. He gripped it firmly in his right hand. He flexed the fingers on his left hand, which held a small but heavy rock. Tucker was poised and ready to fire if necessary.

Hero was similarly primed. The points of his ears rose up, and his nose crinkled as he sorted out the thousands of scents he was catching. He locked his eyes on the cabin. Hero had sensed something inside.

Tsk tsk. Ben made the sound he had practiced with Perillo the night before. It worked. Hero sat down, and Ben knew he wouldn't run into the cabin—no matter what was inside—unless Ben gave him the command.

Ben studied the small, splintering structure, which was barely bigger than a garden shed. It had small windows at the front, but no glass—just torn curtains fluttering in the night breeze. The place was dark, deserted. It looked like it hadn't seen a human in ages.

Hero sniffed at the air. He looked up at Ben, his eyes begging for a command that would let him run to the shed and find whatever was inside.

Ben looked down at Hero—and then something beyond the dog caught his eye, making him gasp audibly. At first he thought his mind was playing tricks on him, but he looked again, straining his eyes, and that's when he knew for sure: The curtain on the left had stopped fluttering.

It had stopped because someone was holding it still.

Someone who was inside the shack.

Looking out.

A million thoughts burst into Ben's brain at once, but one rose above all the others: Had they been spotted by the person inside?

Before he had a chance to learn the answer, a sound

punctured the silence, making Ben, Tucker, and Hero jump.

It was a voice, floating on the night air. Ben recognized it right away.

It was his dad. And he sounded okay. Hoarse, exhausted, maybe in a little bit of pain—but okay.

"People are out looking for me," Sergeant Landry was saying in a calm, even tone. "It's only a matter of time before they find us, and when they do, they're going to want to throw you in jail. But you can still get out of this if you let me help you."

Ben was flooded with joy. He fought the intense urge to call out for his dad. He bit his lip and watched the cabin for any sign of movement.

"Shut up!" a stranger's voice boomed back.

As if in response to the man's angry tone, a single, sharp *bark* rang out from the shack and echoed around the forest.

Scout.

Hero whimpered and scratched the ground with impatience. He stood up and wriggled with a barely contained urgency to move.

"*Tsk tsk,*" Ben signaled. Hero instantly calmed himself and sat back down.

Ben forced himself to take slow, even breaths while he considered their options. He turned to Tucker, who had his eyes locked on the shack. Without looking down at his hands, Tucker slipped the rock into the rubber strap of the slingshot, pulled back on it, and paused. He turned to Ben.

"Only one guy, right?" Tucker whispered to Ben.

"I think so," Ben replied quietly. They'd only heard one voice that wasn't his dad's, and the shack was small—it would have been tight for three grown men at once.

This was good news and bad news. If there was only one convict in there, that meant Ben's dad wasn't currently outnumbered.

But it also meant that if the other guy wasn't in there, he was out *here*—where Ben, Tucker, and Hero were.

He could be anywhere in the darkness around them.

He could even be watching them right that second.

Ben scanned the trees behind them. He listened for man-made sounds. Nothing. He looked at Hero, who was growing ever more desperate to race down to the shack and get to Ben's dad and Scout.

"*What's taking him so long?*" the man in the shack growled. He sounded furious and scared. A dangerous combination.

"The other guy—they're waiting for him to come back," Ben whispered to Tucker.

Tucker nodded. He squinted, gazing over his slingshot, which was aimed squarely at the window where the man had looked out before.

Tucker's hands were steady.

The seconds ticked by slowly. The man in the shack cursed a few times as Ben's dad tried to talk him down.

"I can only help one of you," Ben's dad said. "Don't you want it to be you? But you have to help me first."

And then it happened: The man grabbed at the curtain, yanked it hard to the side, and stuck his face through the window to look outside.

In one swift movement, Tucker released the rubber strap. The rock sliced silently through the air, and the escaped prisoner let out a yell as it bashed him in the forehead.

Blood spouted from a gash above his right eye, and he clutched at it with a meaty hand. He howled in shock and pain—and fell away from the window. Ben and Tucker heard him hit the ground with a sickening thud.

"He's out!" Ben's dad called from inside.

"Go, Ben!" Tucker instructed Ben. "I'll stay here and keep watch."

"Hero, go get Dad!" Ben commanded.

Ben and Hero raced to the flimsy door. Ben kicked it open. In that filthy, crumbling shack, with splinters of wood spiking up from the floor and the smell of rotting leaves emanating from the very walls, Ben saw the most amazing sight of his life: his dad, crumpled in the corner with his back against the wall, looking up at him with a huge smile of relief on his face.

He was bruised and scratched up. His wrists and ankles were lashed together with rope. He winced as he tried to push himself up from the floor.

Ben's dad was hurt.

But he was alive.

16

"BEN!" HIS DAD'S VOICE WAS FILLED with emotion. "What are *you* doing here?"

"Dad—you're okay!" Ben stepped over the unconscious man on the floor and crossed the tiny space in just a couple of steps. He dropped to his knees and, as best he could with the giant bandage on his arm, began untying the bindings on his dad's wrists. Hero bolted over and licked Sergeant Landry's face.

A blur of movement in the corner caught Ben's eye.

Scout whimpered and darted over to Ben and Hero, his tail up and wagging like crazy.

Hero sniffed and nudged at the younger dog, then licked Scout all over his face.

"Ben," his dad said, his voice growing serious, "we're not safe. There's two of them—the other guy will be back any sec—"

Before he could even finish the sentence, his gaze shifted from Ben's face to something over Ben's shoulder, and his expression grew fierce.

Hero shot up and crouched down into a fighting stance, growling deeply. Scout let out a series of angry barks.

Ben spun around.

Standing by the door, just feet from him, was the second escaped prisoner. He wore a ripped orange prison jumpsuit. His face was scratched and muddy, and he had a wild, desperate look in his eye. A sour smell of sweat and dirt emanated from him.

He was looking at Ben.

And he was holding a gun.

Hero's growl shifted into a low, angry snarl, and he bared his top teeth. This was the most aggressive Ben had ever seen Hero—and it made sense. Never before had he needed to protect both Ben *and* his dad.

This man was after Hero's very heart and soul.

And he had no idea what he was about to encounter.

Ben's heart was pounding with fear. His hands

shook. But he was also strangely calm—as if everything had slowed down and become crystal clear. He was hyperaware of everything around him—his dad's ragged breathing, Hero's protective fury, Scout's big eyes watching the scene intently.

"Hero," Ben said, speaking in a voice as strong and deep as possible through clenched teeth. "Stand down. Stay."

Hero hesitated. He didn't want to obey Ben's commands, but he did.

"Good boy," Ben breathed as Hero sat down and went quiet.

Hero kept his eyes locked on the man by the door, waiting for the slightest sound from Ben's mouth or twitch of Ben's finger to attack.

But if there was anyone in the world, besides his mom and sister, that Ben cared about as much as his dad, it was Hero. There was no way Ben was going to let Hero get hurt—and this man clearly wouldn't hesitate to shoot any of them, human or canine.

"Who the hell are you?" the prisoner snarled at Ben. "And what did you do to him?" He gestured at his fellow escapee with the gun. "He better be alive!" he bellowed.

"He's alive," Ben's dad said calmly. "And there's no need to hurt anyone. This is my son. We'll do whatever you ask us to. We're not going anywhere."

"Shut up," the man said, his voice cold and menacing. "I can't think when you're flapping your gums like that." He waved the gun wildly in their direction.

"Okay," Ben's dad said, holding up his still-bound hands in a sign of compliance. "Whatever you need." He nodded at Ben. Ben dropped to the floor next to him. Hero and Scout stood closely together.

With the tip of one muddy boot, the man nudged at his partner, who was still passed out cold on the floor. No response. The man kicked the wall in frustration. The entire shack shuddered with the blow, and for a second Ben thought it might collapse right on top of them.

"You're gonna pay for this, kid!" the prisoner roared at Ben. He lurched toward them, and Ben flinched. His dad leaned forward, trying to put his own injured body between Ben and the man.

Ben could see the frenzied rage in the man's eyes. His chance to escape was on the line here—and Ben was the one standing in the way.

"I don't know what you did to him," the man spat,

"but he's gonna be real pissed off when he wakes up. So I'll tell you what—you're gonna be the first person he sees when he opens his eyes, and you can tell him yourself what you did. What he does to you in return—well, that's up to him."

Ben's jaw was tightly clenched, and his temples pulsed. He was grateful for his dad's steadying presence beside him.

The prisoner waved his gun in their faces. "I have to go take care of something. I won't be gone long, and if either of you try to leave, I'm gonna catch you, and you're gonna get hurt. Well—whatever part of you isn't hurt already by my friend here." He cracked a nasty grin and waved the gun toward the unconscious man on the ground. "You got me loud and clear?"

Ben and his dad nodded.

"Just to make real sure, I'm gonna have to tie you up."

The man pulled some rope from his back pocket and took a shambling step toward Ben. He leaned down—Ben almost gagged from his stench—and grabbed Ben's wrists. Ben's bandaged arm vibrated with pain, but he clenched his teeth and took short, sharp breaths through his nostrils—anything to prevent this jerk from seeing him in pain.

Ben felt his dad tense up next to him. Even with his hands and feet tied up, he was ready to tear the man apart if he hurt Ben. Hero and Scout snarled softly.

"Leave it, Scout," Ben's dad said under his breath.

"Leave it, Hero," Ben said.

The dogs went quiet, but Ben could see from the corner of his eye that, like his dad, they were still on high alert.

Ben let his arms go limp as the man lashed them together tightly. He wasn't going to fight—not now. Not yet. The rope pinched his skin and cut off the circulation. Ben felt weak from the pain radiating from his wound. But he looked the man right in the eye, daring him to look back.

The man kept his eyes on Ben's wrists, then moved on to Ben's ankles. When he was done, the man stood up, looked Ben square in the eye, and grinned from ear to ear.

"That oughta hold you until I get back, kid." He studied Ben for a long moment. Ben wished he could make himself invisible. "You know what he was in for?" The convict jerked a thumb over his shoulder, at his partner on the ground.

Ben shook his head.

"He held a whole family hostage during a robbery. Kids and all." He let out a sharp snort of laughter. "Tell you the truth—I think he kind of enjoyed it."

And with that, the foul man spun around, stomped out of the tiny cabin, and stormed off into the woods.

Ben exhaled. His dad relaxed.

Hero and Scout started to run after the man.

"Stay!" Ben and his dad shouted at the same time. The dogs froze by the door, staring out into the woods—two loyal sentries.

"Let me try to untie you, Ben," his dad said. "We don't have much time before that one wakes up."

Ben held out his hands, and his dad fumbled at the knot binding Ben's wrists together. He could tell that it was hard for his dad to maneuver his fingers with his own wrists tied up so tight. Ben flinched as the ropes rubbed across his injured wrist.

"What happened to your arm?" his dad asked.

Before Ben could answer, Scout barked angrily, and a figure appeared in the doorway.

"Who's there?" Ben's dad demanded, sitting forward and shielding Ben with his body again.

"It's okay," Ben said. "That's Tucker. He's my friend.

He lives around here and he helped me and Hero find you."

"Hi," Tucker said, stepping into the shack. "I'm glad you're okay, sir." He hopped over the unconscious man on the ground and crouched down next to them. "Let me untie those."

"Thanks, Tucker," Ben's dad said. "And thanks for helping my guys."

"You bet."

"Were you behind the rock that took that one out?" He tipped his head toward the behemoth passed out on the floor.

"Yes, sir. With my slingshot."

"Nice work."

"Thanks."

The man on the floor let out a loud snort and they all jumped. They froze, watching him. He twitched, then went slack again.

"He's gonna wake up soon," Tucker said. He freed Ben's dad's wrists and went to work on Ben's.

"He is," Ben's dad said as he flexed and bent his fingers to get the blood flowing into them again, then untied his own ankles. "We need to hurry—I know what they're planning. They were talking about it

147

earlier when they thought I was asleep. There's a convenience store near the northwest corner of the forest. They're going to rob it for supplies and cash and then head south for Louisiana."

Tucker's mouth dropped open and he loosened his hold on Ben's arms for a second. "Northeast corner of the forest, you said?"

Ben's dad nodded. "You know it?"

"Yeah—yeah—I—I know it," Tucker stammered. He looked like he'd been punched in the gut. "It's"— he sucked in his breath—"it's my family's store. My mom and stepdad are there right now."

Ben's dad pressed his lips together and nodded grimly. He and Ben exchanged a worried glance.

Ben put his hand on Tucker's shoulder. "We've got this," he said. "My dad and Hero are here."

Tucker nodded. "We have to go," he said simply. "Now. We have to get there before he does."

17

TUCKER'S HANDS WERE SHAKING AS HE finally managed
to untie Ben.

Ben shook out his good arm and gently wiggled
the fingers on his injured hand. His dad was rubbing
one arm with the other and moving his feet around.
Ben's limbs were tingling after being tied up for a few
minutes. He couldn't imagine how his dad felt after
being bound with rope for two days.

"Ben—your phone," his dad said. "Do you have it?"

Ben pulled it from his pocket and handed it to
him. "No service."

"We'll have to get out of the woods, then," his dad

said. "Let's go." With a grimace, he tried to get to his knees, but he froze in pain.

"Dad! Are you okay?" Ben scanned his dad for injuries but didn't see any. "What is it?"

"I'm fine, son." His dad exhaled slowly. "It's just my leg—my knee is hurt pretty bad, but I'll be okay."

Ben stood and reached down to help his dad to his feet. He gripped his dad's hand and prepared to lift him up.

"Where do you think you're going?" boomed a deep voice behind him. Ben let go of his dad and spun around. The first escaped prisoner was up on his feet, swaying unsteadily and waving a fist at them. Dried blood crusted his forehead and cheek.

Tucker stepped to Ben's side, and Hero and Scout gathered at his feet. Ben dropped his hand to Hero's collar, soothing—and restraining—his dog. "It's okay, Hero," Ben said softly. "Stay."

Ben had seen one gun tonight, and he had to assume this guy had one too.

He wasn't letting Hero get between him and a bullet.

Ben and Tucker stood shoulder to shoulder. The convict took a stumbling step forward. The boys took a reflexive step backward. A couple more feet and they would step right on Ben's dad, who was still sitting on the floor with his back against the wall.

Then the three of them—and the dogs—would be trapped. The shack was small—there wasn't much space between them, and there was even less room to get away.

The man closed in on them. Adrenaline pumped through Ben's body. Maybe, he realized, he was holding on to Hero's collar to keep himself calm, not the other way around.

The man took one more step. He was so close now that Ben could smell his sour breath and see the pores in his skin.

Ben's foot bumped against his dad's leg behind him.

There was nowhere to go. They were cornered.

Hero strained at his collar. Ben tightened his grip and swallowed hard. He felt Tucker shaking next to him.

Ben felt sick for dragging Tucker into this situation. He had no reason to be here—and now he wasn't going to be able to get to his family, who could be in terrible danger.

The man looming before them reached one arm behind him, grappling for something at his back.

It's a gun, Ben thought. *This is it.* There was no way out.

Ben shut his eyes. He waited.

There was a millisecond of torturous silence. It was broken by the earsplitting sound of splintering wood. Ben opened his eyes, confused—it wasn't the noise he was expecting, and it had come from the wrong direction.

Just as he realized what was happening, Ben felt a force surging up from the ground behind him. He jumped out of the way just in time.

It was his father. He rose to his feet like a wild animal and raised a long, splintered plank over his head. He had ripped it from the wall of the shack, and with an angry roar, he threw himself between Ben and Tucker and toward the convict.

He swung the board in a high arc and brought it down on the man's head with a deep, dull *thwack.*

The man's eyes rolled back in his head, and with a pained moan, he crumpled back onto the floor in a sad heap.

Ben's dad staggered backward and slid down to the dirt floor again.

"Dad!" Ben cried. "Are you okay?"

"I'm fine," his dad said, though he looked to Ben like he was anything but. He was pale as a sheet, with beads of sweat gathering on his forehead. He took short, fast breaths through his nose. "Tie him up, boys," his dad said through gritted teeth.

Ben and Tucker grabbed the ropes they had just removed from Ben and his dad, and quickly bound the man's hands and feet.

"You guys need to get out of here," Ben's dad said. "You have to go get help before the other one gets to the store."

"We're not leaving you here!" Ben said. "No way."

"Ben, I can't walk right now."

A bolt of fear passed through Ben. His eyes burned. He struggled to keep his emotions in check.

"I'm okay," his dad said. "You just have to trust me and go. Scout will stay with me."

"Dad—"

"Your dad's right," Tucker said. "We can get help faster if we go on our own. We have to hurry. We just have to get far enough out of the woods to get cell service."

Tucker's face was a mask of fear. He was anxious to get to his family.

Ben knew they were right, but he still hated the hard truth: Leaving his dad behind was their best shot at saving him *and* protecting Tucker's family.

Ben looked back at his dad, fighting tears.

"Go, Ben," his dad said. "Take Hero to protect you. Scout and I will be here when you get back."

Ben nodded. "Okay." He turned to the dogs. "Hero, Scout, come." They scrambled immediately to his side, and he dropped to his knees so he was face-to-face with them. "Scout," Ben said, scratching the younger dog behind the ear. "I need you to stay here and watch out for my dad—that's your job now, got it?" Scout whimpered and let out a short bark. "Thanks, buddy."

Hero leaned down to Scout and placed his head on the back of the younger dog's neck. The two dogs stayed that way for a moment, one folded over the other in a show of solidarity. Ben, his dad, and Tucker watched in appreciative silence.

Ben stood up. He looked at Tucker, then down at Hero.

"Hero, come," he said. Hero pulled himself away from Scout and snapped to Ben's side.

With one backward look at his dad on the hard dirt floor, Ben—with a breaking heart but a clear sense of purpose—strode out of the shack and into the dark woods, headed to find help.

18

TUCKER LED THE WAY THROUGH THE woods. He knew the quickest path to his family's store.

The moon had passed behind a cloud, leaving them shrouded in darkness. The only light was the neon glow on Hero's vest and Ben's phone flashlight. He had lost his real flashlight after the snake bit him.

Every few minutes, he checked his phone for service. Nothing. They were still a few miles into the woods.

Tucker wended through the trees and hopped with ease over the roots and rocks that littered the ground. These were his woods—he could navigate them in darkness just as easily as he could in broad daylight.

Ben knew Tucker was anxious to get to the store, but he was still moving steadily, calmly—almost as if there were no urgency at all.

"You can't be in a hurry in the woods," Tucker said. For a second Ben thought he might have spoken his thoughts out loud. But no—that was just Tucker's uncanny ability to know what Ben was thinking.

"What do you mean?"

"I mean the woods are in charge," Tucker said. "Doesn't matter how much of a rush you're in, you have to stay calm and careful all the time. If you get worked up or try to move too fast, you're in trouble. You'll get lost or confused real fast. Calm and steady. That's how you get through these woods."

Ben couldn't argue with that logic. Last year, during the hurricane, he knew there had been moments when one false move could have gotten him hurt, or worse.

"We're going to make it in time, Tucker," Ben said.

"Yeah," Tucker said simply, ducking under a low branch.

Hero darted through the trees. Ben was exhausted. His feet felt like lead, but he was propelled forward by adrenaline and a desperate desire to help Tucker's family the way Tucker had helped his.

Finally, the tree line began to thin out. The air in the woods grew lighter, less damp. They were approaching the edge of the forest.

Ben checked his phone again. He had a signal. "It's working—tell me the address of your family's store," he said. Tucker gave it to him, and Ben fed the information to the 911 dispatcher. He also begged her to send a team to his dad's location as quickly as possible.

Ben clicked off the call and texted his mom four words: *Found Dad. All good.*

Her reply popped up so quickly that he couldn't believe she could type that fast.

I LOVE YOU was her immediate reply.

Love you too. Help coming. Call you soon, he wrote before sliding the phone back into his pocket.

They stepped out of the woods and onto a blacktop road. Tucker immediately broke into a run. "It's a quarter mile from here," he called out over his shoulder. "Follow me."

Ben tried to keep up, though it was harder than he'd realized to run flat out with one arm in a sling. Hero slowed his pace to stay close to him.

The trio arrived at the edge of a parking lot. They

stopped behind a large trash Dumpster, catching their breath and surveying the scene.

From across the lot, the store was lit up in the night like a Christmas tree. Its entire front was a wall of windows, and even from afar, Ben could see row after row of neatly arranged chips and toilet paper and magazines.

He also saw Tucker's mom and stepdad behind the register, their hands high in the air.

Standing across the counter from them was the prisoner, holding a gun. It was pointed straight at them.

Tucker gasped, and Ben put a steadying hand on his shoulder. Hero growled low and long.

The convict took a step toward Tucker's parents. His stepdad moved in front of his mom and held out a hand toward the man with the gun. He looked like he was trying to calm him down. Ben could tell from the prisoner's body language that he was in no mood to be calm.

They needed a plan—fast.

Ben tried to focus. He shut his eyes and took a deep breath. He opened them again.

They couldn't go in the front door—that was clear.

"Is there another door?" he asked Tucker.

"Yeah, in the back." Tucker's voice was tight. He didn't tear his eyes away from the tense scene inside as he spoke.

"Can he see or hear it from where he is?"

Tucker shook his head. "No. It's in another room. It's separated by a door that's always closed."

"That's good." Ben mapped out a plan. "Here's what we're going to do . . ."

Within minutes, Ben and Hero had moved around the perimeter of the building and positioned themselves outside the back door. Tucker was ready to head in through the front door, to distract the man holding his parents hostage.

Ben fumbled with the key ring Tucker had given him. He slipped the back door key into the lock and took a long, slow breath. *Focus,* he told himself. *Breathe.* He looked down at Hero.

"You ready, buddy?"

Hero gazed up at him with his steady brown eyes. He stood with his four legs perfectly aligned and his head cocked, poised to move at Ben's command. Hero's ears were up and back, and his nostrils flared with short, quick breaths.

They were ready.

Ben reached for the handle of the metal door and pulled it open.

He and Hero stepped into a narrow stockroom lined from floor to ceiling with shelves. Directly ahead of them, another door led into the store.

"Please, sir," Ben heard a man saying calmly. "Take whatever you need. My wife and I are not going to cause you any trouble at all."

"You'd better not!" the other man hollered. "Not if you know what's good for you!"

"We gave you the cash already. Just tell us what else you need and we can get it for you."

"You stay right where you are or I—" The man stopped mid-sentence. "What the— Who are you? Where the heck did you come from?"

"Tucker!" a woman's voice cried out in surprise and fear.

Tucker was inside—that meant the man was distracted and facing the front of the store. It was time for Ben and Hero to move.

"Hero, go!" Ben said softly as he eased open the door leading into the store. They moved through together.

It all happened at once.

Ben pointed down an aisle to his left, giving Hero the hand signal to run that way. Hero shot off down the aisle toward the front of the store.

Ben stepped into the open aisle that ran along the back of the store.

"Hey!" he shouted at the man with the gun. The convict spun around at the sound of Ben's voice. There was a wild, frantic look in his eye—Ben could tell that their campaign of confusion was working.

"You don't learn, do you, kid?" He pointed the gun at Ben. "I thought I made myself clear back there. This is no business of yours—just stay out of it."

"The cops are on their way," Ben shouted, his voice strong and steady—though his heart was trying to escape from his chest, and he had broken out in a cold sweat.

Ben kept his eyes locked on the man's face, but in the background, he saw Tucker take a step toward his parents. Tucker's mom reached under the counter and pulled out a baseball bat.

Just then, Hero rounded the corner behind the convict at top speed. Ben heard the sound of his claws on the linoleum floor just before the man did. In the millisecond after he registered the sound behind him, the man's expression changed from one of aggression to one of fear. He tried to spin around to face Hero, but it was too late.

Hero had vaulted into the air, lifting off with his back legs. He bared his teeth and snarled, his ears flat against the sides of his head and his front legs extended straight out in front of him. Hero hung suspended in midair for an excruciatingly long moment, until his giant paws made contact with the man's back.

There was a *thunk*, and the man grunted as the air was knocked out of his lungs. He fell forward like a bag of rocks, hitting the ground so hard Ben felt the floor vibrate. The blow knocked the gun from his hand, and it skittered across the floor toward the back of the store—and Ben.

Ben stepped on the gun, instantly stopping its spinning progress, and kicked it behind him into the stockroom. Hero stood on top of the convict, his strong legs pressing down on the man's ribs. He barked and growled at the back of the man's greasy head.

Ben looked past Hero at Tucker and his parents. Their faces registered their relief—and their awe at Hero's amazing takedown. Tucker rushed over to them, and they wrapped one another in a grateful hug.

Ben looked back at Hero, ready to commend his dog for a job well done—but something was wrong.

Hero wasn't steady on his feet. He was slipping and stumbling. His front legs were way higher than his back legs. He was rising up, tipping backward . . .

The man on the ground was clambering to all fours, with Hero on his back—and he was throwing Hero off him.

Hero couldn't catch his balance. He scratched at the man's back and opened his jaws to clamp down on the back of the man's neck, but he couldn't find any purchase. Hero slipped sideways and slammed to the floor. He landed on his side with an awful *thud* and rolled onto his back. His paws stuck straight up in the air as he twisted back and forth and tried to right himself again.

The convict was up on his feet. He was unarmed, but filled with rage—the fury of a man who had been locked up for years and was about to lose his only shot at freedom. He roared like an animal, bunched his hands into fists, and spun to face Tucker and his parents. Ben watched, terrified and helpless, as the prisoner took a few lumbering steps toward them.

Hero was scrambling to his feet on the smooth

floor. Ben knew that Hero wouldn't stop getting back up again, no matter how many times he was down. He knew that his dog was preparing to attack—and after seeing Hero flung aside so easily, as if he were nothing more than a sack of garbage—Ben was terrified he would get hurt.

Just the thought of it was like a kick in the gut.

Without thinking, Ben raced toward the front of the store, ready to put himself between Hero and the prisoner if he had to.

It wasn't more than thirty feet, but by the time he got there, it was too late.

Hero was in the air, hurtling toward the man once more, his jaw open and his razor-sharp teeth aiming for the man's arm. But the convict's reflexes were surprisingly fast. He swung his leg out to the side and toward Hero—a perfectly aimed kick that threatened to crush the dog's ribs.

"No!" Ben screamed. He felt like he was trapped in a bad dream—he could see his destination and was telling his body to move, but he couldn't get his legs to work. Hero was just out of his reach, and Ben couldn't speed up enough to save him.

He waited for his dog's pained cries.

But just as the man's filthy boot was about to make contact with Hero, Ben heard the sound of an object slicing through the air. He turned in time to see Tucker, his lips pressed together in concentration and his brow furrowed with effort.

Tucker swung his mother's bat with all his force.

The sound it made when it connected with the convict's leg was flat and disgusting. It was a sound Ben knew would haunt him forever. But it worked. The man fell to the ground with an agonized cry, and Hero landed safely beyond him.

The man was hobbled. But if Ben thought for a second that would stop this monster, he was wrong.

The convict clambered to all fours and half crawled, half clawed his way toward the door, grunting in pain as he went.

Ben, Tucker, and the others simply stared after him, paralyzed by the man's shocking display of persistence. He threw himself through the front door and into the parking lot, his head swiveling back and forth as he desperately searched for a way to escape.

At just that moment, a car turned into the parking lot. From where he stood inside, Ben saw a woman in the driver's seat, talking and looking in the rearview mirror. Ben followed her gaze and saw a smiling baby waving her arms from a car seat.

"No!" he screamed. *"No no no no no!"*

"Stop him!" Tucker cried.

Tucker and Ben reached the door at the same instant, right as Hero slipped between them and made it outside first. The car turned into the spot closest to the front door. Through the open car window, Ben heard the woman cooing to her daughter, totally unaware of the drama unfolding just steps away.

The man tripped toward her car and reached an arm through her window. Startled, the woman let out a small yelp and clutched at her throat. She tried to roll up the window, but he had already jammed his arm toward the inside door handle. The door swung open, and in one movement, he reached down and unbuckled the woman's seat belt, grabbed her by the arm, and yanked her out of the car. He tossed her to the ground like she weighed nothing.

"My baby!" she screamed as she fell. "Stop! My baby! Please!"

The man ignored her pleas and climbed into the car, slamming the door behind him. He threw the car into reverse and pulled out of the parking spot.

He put it into drive and began to pull away.

"Hero! Go!" Ben commanded. Hero raced toward the car, his body springing up and down as he ran faster than Ben had ever seen him move. At that moment, Tucker stepped forward and raised his arms. He loaded a rock into his slingshot and pulled the band back in one smooth motion, releasing it with a flick of his finger. The projectile sailed over Hero's head and rocketed through the open car window, nailing the man on the temple.

The prisoner cried out in agony, but rather than coming to a stop, he pressed down on the accelerator. The car sped up, careening across the lot.

Hero didn't miss a step.

He zigzagged after the car until he saw his chance and—without hesitation—he took it. Hero kicked off of his back legs and vaulted in a graceful arc through the driver's-side window, landing squarely on the man's head and chest, digging his claws into him.

The car swerved sharply to the right and came to a screeching halt. As he ran toward the car, Ben heard Hero growling and the man moaning.

Sirens rang out in the distance, growing louder by

the second. Tucker's parents ran out of the store, and the four of them crowded together by the car, ready to stop the man if he tried to escape again.

But he wasn't going anywhere this time. He was out cold.

The baby began to cry in the back seat. Her mother ran to the car from across the lot, ripped open the door, and, sobbing, cradled her baby in her arms.

Hero spun around and stuck his head out the driver's-side window, looking right at Ben.

Ben doubled over, overcome with emotion. He put his hands on his knees to steady himself.

When his heart rate began to slow, Ben looked up at his dog.

"Atta boy, Hero," Ben said. "Good job."

19

RED AND BLUE LIGHTS FLOODED THE parking lot in alternating flashes. Voices crackled and popped on squad car radios. Policewomen and -men scurried back and forth collecting evidence. Two officers jogged alongside a gurney carrying the escaped prisoner, who was handcuffed to the metal bars. They loaded him into a waiting ambulance and sped off.

Ben sat with Hero in the back of another ambulance, his legs dangling over the bumper. Hero rested his head in Ben's lap while Ben let the EMTs bandage up his cuts and scrapes, and clean and dress the snakebite on his wrist. But all the while he looked over their shoulders, waiting for word about his dad.

A squad car turned quickly into the lot and came to a stop a few feet away. Officer Perillo hopped out and ran to Ben.

"Thank God you're okay!" she cried. "Ben—you scared us all half to death."

"My dad—" Ben began.

Perillo smiled. "He's fine, Ben. You did good."

Ben let out a choked sob of relief.

"Our guys picked him up a few minutes ago," Perillo went on. "He's going to meet you at the hospital. And they got the other convict while they were there. Good job tying him up, by the way."

"Thank you, Officer Perillo," Ben exhaled, tears filling his eyes. "Thank you so much—for everything."

"You got it, Ben." She put a hand on his shoulder—and pressed down pretty hard. It was more like a warning than for comfort. "Sit tight," she said with a knowing grin. "I mean it this time. Your mom will be here any second."

As she said it, another police car raced down the road and pulled into the lot. The car had barely slowed to a stop when Ben's mom and little sister flew out of the back seat. Within seconds, Ben and Hero were being smothered with hugs and kisses and sniffles. Ben felt his mom's arms wrapped tightly around his shoulders. Erin and Hero were squished between them.

Hero wriggled and wagged his tail to a fast beat, and Ben sucked in his breath to contain the flood of emotions he felt at seeing his family again.

"Dad's okay!" he said, his voice muffled in his mom's shoulder.

"I know, sweetie," she said, stroking his hair. "I know. We're going to see him in a minute."

She grabbed Ben by the shoulders and pushed him away gently but firmly.

"Honey," she began, wiping the tears on her cheeks with the back of her hand. "You're safe, and your dad is going to be all right. That's the most important thing. But, Ben—" Her voice cracked. She took a couple of quick breaths and composed herself. "Ben, you scared me. Again."

"Benny," Erin said as she clutched his arm tightly with her little fingers. "Don't ever do that again."

Ben and his mom burst out laughing through their tears.

"Okay, Sis," Ben said, rubbing her head. He wiped away the tears leaking from the corners of his eyes and turned to his mom. "Mom, I—" He didn't know where to begin. What was there to say? After all they had been through as a family . . . "I just— Mom, I just can't sit by when someone I love is in trouble—when anyone is in trouble. I can't let it happen when there's something Hero and I can do to help."

His mom gazed at him for a long moment and tucked his hair behind his ear. He didn't roll his eyes and swat her away, like he normally would. She nodded and smiled.

"I know, Ben," she said. "You are truly your father's son. But you're still so young. We just have to figure out what to do for the next four or so years."

Ben tilted his head and looked at her, confused. "Four years? What do you mean?"

"Well," his mom said with a resigned exhale, "you're almost fourteen. And you're not allowed to join the police academy until you're eighteen, so we're going to have to find something to keep you busy—and safe— until then."

Hero dropped his head back into Ben's lap, and Erin climbed onto the back of the ambulance, put her head down on Hero's chest, and reached for Ben's hand. Ben's mom stretched out her arms and enveloped all three of them in a great big hug.

Ben felt Hero's warm fur under his palm, his sister's little hand on his, and his mom's firm grip on his shoulder.

"Thank you" was all Ben could say.

20

"GET UP."

Ben opened his eyes.

Noah stood over the lower bunk with a serious scowl on his face and a bag of warm bagels in his hand. Jack stood behind him, shaking his head at Noah.

"You need carbs," Noah said, dropping the bag onto Ben's bed. "And you need to get up and practice before the game."

"Thanks," Ben said, rubbing his eyes.

Tucker rolled over on the top bunk and stuck his head over the side. "Morning, Noah," he mumbled. "Morning, Jack."

"Morning," Jack said apologetically. "Sorry about Noah's charm offensive here."

"Let's go, fellas," Noah said. "I don't have all day. Oh, wait—I do have all day. Because I have nothing else to do." He held up his arm in its stiff white cast.

Ben buried his head under his pillow. He spoke through the stuffing.

"So, we literally saved a whole bunch of lives, helped catch a couple of escaped felons—oh, and I got bitten by a snake and Tucker's parents got held up at gunpoint—but you're still upset about your broken arm and one game?"

Noah thought for a second.

"Yep," he said with a shrug.

"All right, then. Guess we'd better practice, Tucker," Ben said. "Let's do it for poor Noah here."

Tucker hopped down from the top bunk and stretched out.

It was hard to believe it had been just five days since he and Tucker had trekked into the woods with Hero.

When he got home, Ben never thought his wrist would heal fast enough to pitch in the playoff game.

But here he was.

With Tucker.

Somehow, during their epic trek through the woods, their shared love of baseball hadn't come up—and Tucker had never brought up the fact that he was an ace pitcher and the captain of his school team.

Tucker's parents had decided he'd earned a little time off from school. Once Tucker learned about Ben's pitching dilemma—and realized just how much help he needed to get ready for the playoff game—he had decided to come back to Gulfport with Ben.

Tucker, Noah, and Jack had been training Ben all week, pushing him as hard as the doctor would allow.

They had only a couple more hours to go over a few final pointers. Ben stumbled out of bed, ran his hands through his hair, and stretched out his stiff body. Hero got to his feet too, his tag clinking against his collar. He sniffed at Noah's cast, and Noah scratched him under the chin with his good hand.

"Good morning, Hero," Noah said. Scout scurried over from the corner and rubbed up against Noah's legs. "Good morning, Scout."

"Make yourself useful and feed those two, would you?" Ben grumbled at his friend.

Noah held up his cast again. "Sorry. Can't do that. Doctor's orders."

"Right," Ben said, heading out his bedroom door. "Doctor's orders."

Just hours later, Ben squinted into the sunlight. He shook out his pitching arm and squeezed the ball in his fist a few times. He turned sideways, eyed the batter carefully, nodded at his catcher, drew in his knee, and pulled his arm back, poised to throw the ball.

But first he paused. He turned his head ever so slightly and scanned the bleachers until he found what he was looking for.

There they were.

He put his fingers to the brim of his baseball cap and tipped it in their direction.

Ben caught Tucker's eye. Tucker raised his right arm up, rotated his wrist sideways, and mimed pitching a ball—signaling Ben to go with the slider.

Ben nodded.

"You got this, Ben," Jack called out from a few yards off to his left, where he crouched at first base.

There was no way around it—Ben wanted to win this game. The pitch he was about to throw could be the deciding play. And he was ready.

But whether he won or lost wouldn't change the most important thing about Ben's life: Everyone he loved was gathered together and watching him from the stands.

His dad, mom, and sister sat side by side on a metal bench with Tucker, his mom and stepdad, and Noah and his parents. Jack's mom was right there with them.

Ben's dad was bandaged up, and his knee was in a stiff brace—but he was going to be fine. Next to him, Officer Perillo and her daughter waved their hands in the air and let out a loud holler.

At their feet, Scout watched the game with big eyes and his full attention, his head swiveling back and forth as the ball flew around the field.

And next to Scout sat Hero, serene, focused, and alert. Ben could feel his dog's watchful gaze on his every move.

Ben looked at Hero for a long moment, then turned back toward the batter. He released a perfect sideways pitch that snuck over home plate at the last second. The batter swung—and got nothing but air.

"Strike three!" the umpire called out.

The crowd went nuts. Just before his teammates swooped in and carried him to the dugout on their shoulders, Ben heard his family and friends whistling and yelling his name.

Louder and clearer than all of them, Hero howled in celebration, his beautiful cry filling Ben's ears.

Hero, buddy, Ben thought, *this one's for you.*

ACKNOWLEDGMENTS

Hero, Scout, and I are lucky to have such an amazing team: Les Morgenstein, Josh Bank, Sara Shandler, and Romy Golan at Alloy; Margaret Anastas, Luana Horry, and the sales, marketing, and publicity groups at Harper; and Katelyn Hales at the Robin Straus Agency. Thanks to you all!

Hayley Wagreich and Robin Straus, thank you for walking, feeding, and training me.

And what's a writer—or a dog—without a family? My love and thanks to Brian, the goons, Virginia Wing, Kunsang Bhuti, and now . . . Vida the rescue superpup! I look forward to many heroic adventures together.